The Black Book

[DIARY OF A TEENAGE STUD]

VOL. IV

Faster, Faster, Faster

■

JONAH BLACK

AVON BOOKS
An Imprint of HarperCollins*Publishers*

The Black Book [Diary of a Teenage Stud], Vol. IV:
Faster, Faster, Faster

Cover Photograph from Tony Stone
Design by Russell Gordon

Printed in the United States of America.

For information address
HarperCollins Children's Books, a division of
HarperCollins Publishers, 1350 Avenue of the Americas,
New York, NY 10019.

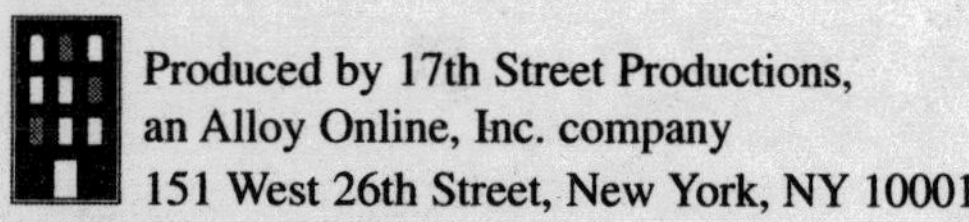

Library of Congress Catalog Card Number: 2001116877
ISBN 0-06-440801-9

First Avon edition, 2002

AVON TRADEMARK REG. U.S. PAT. OFF.
AND IN OTHER COUNTRIES,
MARCA REGISTRADA, HECHO EN U.S.A.

Visit us on the World Wide Web!
www.harperteen.com

Faster, Faster, Faster

Jan. 11, 9 A.M.

I looked over at Molly, and she stuck her tongue out at me. I was glad we were next to each other. Her hair was hanging loose, and she kept pushing it back behind her ears and licking her lips. I wanted to lean over to her and say, "Don't be nervous. It's going to be okay," but they yell at you if you talk during the SATs. I was supposed to be concentrating on my own test, not on Molly.

I looked down at my left arm. Doing the SAT while wearing a cast was a pain in the ass. It's so big and clunky, I kept almost knocking my test booklet off the desk, and it was hard to hold onto the answer sheet while I filled in the bubbles with my right hand. It still says: MARRY ME, JONAH in big letters on the side of my cast. I wish Molly had written it. That

—■—

would have made my life much less confusing. But I know it wasn't her. It was Northgirl999 from the Internet. And I still don't know who she is.

The proctor was Miss von Esse, my German and homeroom teacher. She cleared her throat and said, "Please write your names on the answer sheet. After you write your names, enter in all the other information. When you are finished, look up at me so I'll know you're ready to move on."

I wrote my name in the space. *Jonah Black.* I wrote down my address and my hometown, *Pompano Beach, Florida.* Then I wrote down the code for Don Shula High School. I guess one of the few good things about getting kicked out of boarding school, and being sent home to Florida, and having to repeat the eleventh grade, is getting another chance at the SAT. I need all the help I can get.

When I finished filling out the information on the answer sheet, I looked up at Miss von Esse, but she wasn't looking at me. I looked over at Molly. She crossed her eyes and stuck her tongue out again. I guess she thought she was being funny, but it was kind of distracting. All of the junior and senior girls from St. Winnifred's were taking their SATs at Don Shula High, along with the girls from the other Catholic girls' school, Sacred Heart. Because of that there were about three times more girls in

---

the Don Shula auditorium than guys. Which was fine with me, although it definitely made it hard to concentrate on antonyms. I saw where Molly colored in the little circle on the Address section of her answer sheet marked *F*. I looked down at mine, where I'd colored in the circle marked *M*, and then back over at the Molly's answer sheet again. Her eraser was moist.

Molly winked at me and stuck her eraser in her mouth again, rolling it around on her tongue. Then she takes it out and traces a heart on my cheek. She kisses me where she's drawn the heart. Sophie's wrists are so delicate, and her hands flutter like little bird wings around my face. "I love you, Jonah Black," says Sophie, before she flies away.

"This first section of the test will take twenty-five minutes," Miss von Esse said. "When you finish this first section, you may go back and review your work. Do not go on to other sections. Are you ready?"

Molly ran her tongue around the edges of her lips.

"All right. Begin!" Miss von Esse said.

We opened up the seals on our test booklets and began the SAT. My first test was in math, which was good. I like math.

Two trains are headed toward Kennebunkport,

—— ■ ——

Maine, at different speeds. Train A starts 660 miles away and is traveling at 45 miles per hour. Train B is 450 miles away and is . . . etc. For a few minutes I got all Zen with the math problems, filling in the bubbles like clockwork. I was feeling good.

Then I glanced over at the girl on my left. She was very tall and thin with stringy brown hair and a big purple bruise on her knee, as if she'd taken a bad fall. Fell off her bike, maybe. It looked like it hurt. I looked back at her face, but now Sophie O'Brien is sitting in her seat instead. She doesn't have a test booklet. She is just sitting there, chewing on a strand of her golden blond hair.

Sophie looks over at me with sad, sad eyes, and whispers, "Help me, Jonah." The diamond studs in her ears glitter in the fluorescent lights of the auditorium.

I swallowed the lump in my throat and turned back to my test. *A team hasn't won 80% of the 35 games it has played against State. The team has lost 25% of the nine games it has played against City University. If the team plays four more games against State and five more games against City University and continues its percentage of wins and losses against each, how many games will the team have won for the season?*

I read this a couple of times, but I couldn't get it

—■—

to gel. I felt my heart beating quickly. *Focus, Jonah,* I told myself. *Focus.* On my left, I heard someone whimper softly. I looked over and there's Sophie again, crying. "Jonah, please. Save me."

I forced myself to go back to my test. In the next question they gave us a drawing of a rectangular solid and the length of three of the sides. We were supposed to find out the volume of the solid. I know I knew how to do that, but I started to panic. I was like, *I can't do it, I'm going to freak out.* So I went on to the next question.

The square root of an integer x *is twice the square root of a negative real number* y. *If* z *= 3*x *and* x *= 7/5ths* z, *what is the square root of . . .*

From my left I hear her whisper again. "Jonah," she says urgently. "Jonah!"

Sophie's eyes are huge and filled with tears. "Sophie," I whisper. "What are you *doing* here?"

"I had to come see you," she says. She rubs her bruised knee and pushes her hair back behind her ears. "I need to talk to you."

"Aren't you supposed to be in—?" I say. "I mean I thought you were in Maggins—you know, the—"

"The loony bin," Sophie says.

"I don't know what you call it," I said.

"The looooooooooo-ny bin," she says, like it's funny.

—— ■ ——

"Whatever."

"Jonah," she says, leaning toward me. "I wanted to say I'm sorry. About what happened."

I put my pencil down. "You mean over Christmas break?" I say.

"Yeah." She wipes her nose with the back of her hand. "I mean, it was so nice of you to rent a hotel room so we could be together. I know it was like, a risk, for us to actually meet and everything. And I'm sorry I took off like that. I'm kind of screwed up," she says. "But I guess you figured that out. That's why they put me in Maggins."

"I don't care if you're screwed up," I say.

"I'm totally in love with you, Jonah," she says. "Did I tell you that? You're my hero."

I heard a guy clear his throat, and I looked over at him. It was Thorne, my best friend. He was taking his SAT for like, the fifth time. He just wants to make sure he won't be gutting fish on his dad's boat his entire life. I don't blame him. Thorne pointed at his test booklet and mouthed the words, *Jonah, dude. Concentrate.*

I looked down at my test. Most of the bubbles on my answer sheet were still not filled in. I glanced over to my left. The girl with the bruise was scribbling away. Sophie had disappeared.

Miss von Esse jiggled her bracelets and I blushed.

I was going to wind up working for Thorne's dad for the rest of my life if I didn't start filling in my answers.

But I still couldn't concentrate. Posie was sitting two desks in front of Thorne, working hard. She couldn't see me. Her shirt had a big neck and one side of it had fallen off her shoulder. I could see the straps of her orange bikini top underneath.

I remembered the time Posie and I were out in her little boat all night long, making out. We'd forgotten to drop the anchor, so we'd just drifted around for hours. Thorne and his dad had to rescue us.

I hate how I hardly see Thorne and Posie around anymore. The fact that I'm a junior now and they're seniors doesn't help. But ever since Posie started going out with Lamar Jameson, she doesn't have much time for anybody else. And Thorne's always got his hands full with like, five girls at once. If he messes up the SAT and doesn't get into a decent college, he could make money teaching courses on how to be a player. He has it down to a science.

To my left, someone smacks her hand on the desk. I look over and Sophie looks back at me, annoyed. *"Hello?"* she says. "Do you *mind*?"

"Mind what?" I say.

"Like, focusing on the situation?" she says.

"You mean the SAT?" I say.

"No, no, no," Sophie says, shaking her head like I'm hopeless. "I mean *my* situation. *Me.* What are you going to do about *me*?"

"Sophie," I say. "Now is not such a good time. I'm supposed to be doing this test."

Sophie gets up and sits down on top of my desk. She takes out one of her earrings, which is one of the ones I gave her in Disney World, then she kisses it, and puts it on top of my answer sheet. "I don't think so," she says.

"Oh," I say, confused.

"Jonah," she says, as if she's getting tired of explaining things to me. "When are we going to do it?"

"Do it?" I say.

"Yeah, do it." She licks her lips. "How much longer am I going to stay a virgin for you? I can't wait forever, you know. And what about you? You can't tell me you don't want to do it with me, can you? I mean, how long can we stay virgins?"

My hands feel cold and sweaty. "Okay," I say.

Sophie gets a tube of lip gloss out of her purse and rubs some on her lips.

"So let's do it," she says. "Come on. Let's go."

Suddenly she drops the lip gloss and it rolls across the floor. She watches it with wide, frightened eyes, as if she's just dropped a grenade, and then tears begin to stream down her cheeks.

"Sophie!" I cried.

I heard my voice echo in the auditorium. Everyone stared at me, even Posie. Molly glared at me fiercely. I think she knew exactly what had happened.

"Mr. Black," Miss von Esse said. I shook my head and looked down at my SAT. I was only on question nine. Everyone else was nearly finished with the section. This is exactly what happened when I took my SAT last year up at boarding school.

I went back to my test and everyone started working again. *A right triangle with a side of 37 inches has one angle of 48 degrees. If the hypotenuse is 47 inches long, what is the degree of . . .*

I thought I could still smell Sophie's shampoo. It smells like honey and daisies.

"All right, stop working," says Sophie.

She is sitting on Miss von Esse's desk, unbuttoning her shirt with her birdlike fingers.

"Jonah Black, she says. "Will you please come to the front of the room and help me?"

(Later.)

"Let me guess," Molly said, as she drove me home in her Dad's Expedition. "You started daydreaming about Sophie again. You were imagining

—— ■ ——

her taking her top off in the chair next to you."

I looked out the window. "Something like that," I said.

"Something like that?" said Molly. "Okay, was it worse than that?"

"Sort of."

"Goddammit," Molly said. The tires of her SUV screeched as we went around a corner and bounced over the curb. Man, is she a bad driver—worse than me, even. Of course, she has a license and I don't. I don't even have a bicycle because Molly crushed mine with that monster SUV of hers, just to get my attention. In fact, I haven't been able to deliver any pizzas or videos in like, a week. I wonder if Mr. Swede is going to fire me.

"What exactly were you thinking?" Molly asked, speeding up to shoot through a light that was just turning red.

"I don't want to talk about it," I said.

Molly slammed on the brakes. Behind us, tires squealed and horns honked. Molly gave them the finger and put on her hazard flashers. Driving with her is always a thrill.

"Listen," said Molly. "You want me to throw you out of this car? I told you if we were going to hang out you were going to have to tell me the truth. About everything. That's the way I operate. Okay? No lies,

—— ■ ——

no crap, no bullshit. So tell me what you were thinking, or else I'm letting you out."

"I kept hearing Sophie asking for my help," I explained. I knew I couldn't lie to her, because she'd figure it out. I hate the way Molly always knows what I'm thinking, or at least thinks she does. We haven't really even started going out yet, but I have a feeling that the longer I know her, the more this is going to bother me. There's nothing wrong with keeping some things to yourself.

We'd stopped right in the middle of Federal Highway. People were driving around us, shaking their fists at us or giving us the finger. Molly didn't seem to care. She just sat there behind the wheel, her slightly dirty-brown hair tucked behind her ears, her little gold seashell earrings reflecting the Florida sunlight, looking smarter than everyone else in the world. She really is kind of cute.

"Stop it," Molly said.

"Stop what?"

"Stop imagining me with my clothes off. I'm trying to have a fight with you."

"Sorry," I said.

She turned off her hazard lights, put the Expedition back in gear, and started driving toward my house again.

—— ■ ——

"So, she was asking you to help her?" Molly asked.

"Yeah."

"And you were in this little trance, how long?" she asked.

"I don't know. Long enough to screw up one of the math sections."

"Jesus, Jonah. I thought you'd concluded that Sophie was a fruitcake. I thought you were over her."

"I am," I said, although I admit it sounded kind of weak.

"Then how come you were thinking about her in the middle of your SATs?" Molly challenged.

I watched the palm trees waving in the warm sunshine. We passed the airport. Then we passed the hangar for the Goodyear Blimp, but the blimp wasn't there.

"Because she's in trouble," I explained. "Because she's in this mental institution or whatever. Because she wrote me a letter asking me to come and save her."

"So what are you going to do? You can't go all the way up to Pennsylvania and rescue her. You don't even have a driver's license. Besides, what would you do when you got there? Like, break into the nuthouse, overpower the guards, and do it

———■———

with Sophie on top of the electroshock table or something?" Molly said. She rolled her eyes. "Please."

"I don't know," I said, looking out the window again.

"Man," Molly said. She sounded incredibly disappointed in me. "Man."

"Listen, I know Sophie's nuts," I said. "It's just that when I got that letter from her, asking me to save her, she said I was the only person in the world she could go to for help. It's just hard to get a letter like that and to do nothing. I mean, what would you do if you got a letter like that?"

"What would I do?" Molly said. She was driving down the middle of the road, straddling the yellow line. "Good question. I'll tell you what I'd do. I'd realize that this girl has some serious problems. I'd realize that a mental institution is probably the best place for her. I'd figure out that the problems Sophie has are not ones I can solve. I'd let the professionals help her, and I'd stay out of it.

"You know what else? I'd realize I could be about to hook up with this incredibly intelligent, beautiful girl named Molly—*that's me*—and I'd start concentrating on *her*. Because if I don't, Molly might throw me out of her Expedition and break my other arm."

———■———

I shook my head. "You know, Molly," I said. "We haven't exactly hooked up yet."

"You mean, we haven't had sex, right? Oh, no. We're not going fight about this, are we?" Molly asked.

"I don't want to fight with you about it," I said. "I just wish you wouldn't dismiss it so quickly."

Molly laughed. "Oh, Jonah. Sex isn't important."

This is what annoys me the most. Molly claims she's had sex lots of times before and it's really no big deal. But if that's true, then what's the big deal about doing it with me?

"If it's not important, then why can't we do it?" I insisted.

"Jonah, believe me. You're not missing anything," she said. She flicked on the squirter and wiped the windshield clean. She was driving so slowly now, I was worried we were going to get arrested for going under the speed limit.

"I wish you'd let me decide that for myself," I said.

"I'm serious," Molly said, turning into my driveway. "Sex is overrated."

"Whatever," I said.

Molly missed the driveway completely, crushing one of my mother's azaleas.

"Okay, Mommy's waiting to make you lunch,"

———■———

she said. "You better go in there and tell her how you screwed up your SATs."

"You know, you didn't tell me how *you* did on the SATs," I said.

"Are you kidding?" Molly said. "*Easy*. Hey, you know what I'm going to do when I get out of college?"

"I don't know. Teach driver's ed, maybe?"

"No way," she said. "I'm gonna *write* SATs."

"I think you'd be a better driving teacher," I said.

Molly grabbed me by the back of the head and kissed me on the mouth. Her lips tasted like pencil eraser. "Aw," she said. "You're just saying that."

"Yeah," I admitted.

"Can I ask you a serious question?" she said. "How come you never fantasize about *me* when you have these little breakdowns? Why do you have to fantasize about that mental case? I mean, you've *got* me, Jonah Black." Then she whacked herself on the forehead. "Duh! I guess I just answered my own question."

I was thinking, *Maybe if we had sex I'd fantasize about you all the time.* But I didn't say it.

I got my backpack and opened the car door. "Okay," Molly said. "Don't forget to tell your Mom she's a phony."

—■—

"Okay. Want me to call you later?" I said.

"You'd better," said Molly, and then she drove off. There was a huge tire mark across the flower beds.

I went inside and found Mom and my history teacher on the floor in these weird yoga positions. They were kind of standing on their heads, with their knees bent and their feet touching.

"Rommm," chanted Mr. Bond.

"Rommm," Mom chanted in response.

"Hi," I said.

"Sshh," said Mom. "You're disturbing the *poon*."

"Aahh . . . Aahh . . ." said Mr. Bond, like he was about to sneeze.

"The what?" I said.

"The *poon*," said Mom.

Mr. Bond suddenly fell over and lay on the floor, looking dazed.

Mom came down from her headstand and sat up.

"It's a kind of energy," Mom explained. She stroked Mr. Bond's cheek. "Are you okay, Robere?"

"I'm all right," he said. "Boy, was I tranquil!"

"You think I can use this one in my book?" Mom asked. She picked up a stack of Post-it notes and started writing on one.

"Definitely," Mr. Bond said. "*Poon* energy is kind

of hard to describe though. It's like a spiral that gets wider and deeper the higher you go."

My mother nodded thoughtfully and took more notes.

"You're still writing a new book, Mom?" I said.

"Of course I am, Jonah," Mom said. "It's called *Hello Pleasure! Dr. Judith Black's Guide to Being Nice to Yourself.*"

"Sounds like another best-seller, Mom," I said.

Mr. Bond looked down at a chart he had opened on the floor. There were lots of drawings of nude people in weird positions. "Now this next one is called *Tanngghh.*"

"Tanngghh?" Mom said, looking at the chart.

"Okay, first I put my hands on your *schmeng,*" said Mr. Bond.

He put his hands on Mom's breasts.

"That's called *schmeng*?" I said.

"It's an energy field," Mom explained matter-of-factly.

I could not get out of there fast enough. Mom and Mr. Bond are like explorers, in a way. Every time I think they've gotten as weird as they're going to get, it's like they discover a whole new territory of strangeness. They're like the Lewis and Clark of weirdness.

I went into the kitchen and got a bag of Doritos

---

and a glass of Coke and went into my room. Honey was lying on my bed, looking up at the ceiling. She was wearing her metal-studded dog collar, a black bra, and overalls, and she was listening to her Discman.

"Honey," I said.

She looked over at me.

"Be with you in a minute," she said. She looked at her nails, which were painted black.

"Honey," I said again.

She took off the headphones. Loud music sprayed out of them. It was Mudvayne, I think. Seriously hard core.

"What?" she said. She looked annoyed.

"What are you doing in my room?" I said.

"I don't know. I like it in here," she said. I noticed that on my dresser was a weird assortment of objects: a skull with a candle burning in it, a balloon tied to a string that went around the neck of a doll with no arms or legs, and a ruler balanced on the edge of a glass. Way up on a high shelf was a plastic cup of soda with a string tied around it.

"What the hell is all this stuff?" I demanded.

"It's part of an experiment I'm doing, Peanut Brain," Honey said. She picked up a pad of yellow legal paper she had on the bed. "I'm about to do an experiment. I have to take notes."

"Do you mind doing it in your room?" I said.

"Aw, get over yourself, Flounder Nuts." Honey turned off her music. "I was just trying to figure some things out. I thought maybe your room would be better than mine. Since you're the big thinker and everything."

"What are you trying to figure out?" I asked.

"What do you care?" she said. She handed me a letter she had with her on the bed. "I got this from Harvard." I looked at it—it was a form with lots of personal questions on it. "They want to know my preferences in roommates. Like, do I want a smoker, or a vegetarian, or a lesbian, or what."

"You can request all of that?" I said.

"Hey, big brother," she said. "It's Harvard. You can request whatever the hell you want." She took the paper back from me. "Listen to this. 'Are you spiritual? Are you political? What kind of music do you listen to? Do you have any pets?' "

"So what are you requesting?"

"A single," she said.

"I think that's probably a good idea, for everybody," I said. "That way nobody gets hurt."

"People are getting hurt," she said. "I just haven't figured out who yet."

"So that's what you're trying to figure out?" I asked.

"That and about a million other things. I'm multitasking," Honey replied. She drew an *X* on my white pillowcase with her blue pen.

"Well, listen. Do you think you could multitask in your room?" I said. I just wanted to be left alone."

"Jonah, I could multitask in my sleep," she said. "Hey, you want to take a road trip with me next week? I'm going to drive up to Harvard to talk to some professors. I might stop in Pennsylvania and tell our father what a jerk he is while I'm at it."

"You're serious? You're driving all the way up to Massachusetts?"

"Of course I'm serious. I've already gotten into college. There's nothing to do this semester except drive the teachers at Don Shula insane. And I think we can safely consider that mission accomplished." Honey smirked.

"When exactly would this road trip be?" I asked.

Honey sat up, put my pillow in her lap, and punched it a few times. "I don't know, maybe leave Saturday, be up there by Monday, yell at Dad that night, then head up to Boston on Tuesday, look around Cambridge on Wednesday, head south Thursday or Friday, back home, hmm, maybe around 3:45 A.M. on Sunday morning?"

—■—

"Why don't you just *fly* up to Boston for a couple of days?" I said.

"Jonah," she said. "You're asking me why I'd prefer a road trip to flying USAir? Like, why I'd rather be in a Jeep listening to Mudvayne instead of in coach class with somebody's baby taking a dump in my lap?"

I thought about going with her. I wouldn't mind seeing Dad. I hadn't seen him since I got kicked out of Masthead Academy.

The second I thought of Masthead, though, I thought of Sophie. And Maggins. Which wasn't more than ten minutes from Dad's house in Bryn Mawr. I could go up there and rescue her.

"Oh, no," said Honey, getting up. "I don't like that look."

"What look?" I said, innocently.

"You're scheming. Coming up with something. I don't even want to know what."

"I was just thinking about the two of us on the road together. Really."

"Yeah, right." Honey said. "Okay, Wormhead, watch."

Honey picked up a rubber band that was lying on my night table, wrapped it around her index finger, and shot it toward my dresser. The rubber band burst the balloon, and the quarter taped to the bottom of it fell onto one end of a ruler that she'd set up like a seesaw. The ruler tipped on the edge of the glass and raised the skull with the candle which was balanced on the other end so that the flame of the candle burned through a piece of string. When the string broke, a weight tied to the other end of it crashed to the floor and pulled the plastic cup of soda off of the top of my bookcase and onto my head.

"Christ!"

"Okay, hang on," Honey said. "I have to write down everything you say right now. You know, as part of the experiment. I have to record it exactly."

"Get out of my room!" I shouted, throwing the empty plastic cup at her.

"Wait, you're talking too fast," Honey said, scribbling on the pad. "Get . . . out . . . of . . . Okay, wait, what was the rest?"

"Honey," I said, stepping toward her. "I am about to kill you."

"Oh, all right, Bonehead." she said, getting up. "You know, this is what people said to Thomas Smartypants Edison, too."

"Alva," I said. "His middle name was Alva."

"Right," Honey said. "You believe *that*?"

She started walking out of my room but paused by the door. There was a stack of CDs on my

———■———

bureau. Honey reached out and grabbed the whole stack.

"And these are mine," she said. "Okay?"

"I just borrowed them," I said, lamely.

"Okay, Monkey Boy," she called, walking down the hall. "Next time, stay out of *my* room."

—■—

Jan. 12

Today I went to the hospital to see Pops Berman, but when I got there they said he'd been released. Pops has always been the one person who gives it to me straight when it comes to girls, and I could use some advice. But he's home now, I guess. I thought about going over to Niagara Towers to see him, but by then I wasn't in the mood. The hospital was just too depressing. I keep hoping I'll see him down by the lifeguard stand like I used to, but he doesn't come down there anymore. I have a feeling he's really sick, and that makes me sad.

(Still Jan. 12, 11 P.M.)

I just got off the phone with Molly. I think she was feeling bad about being so bitchy to me yesterday.

---■---

When she called I was about to go online to see if Northgirl was on. I felt kind of guilty, like I was about to cheat on Molly, even thought we're not really going out yet.

First, Molly said she was sorry.

"It's just that I hate seeing you with your head in the clouds all the time," she said. "There's a lot of cool stuff down here on the ground, you know?"

"Like what?" I said.

"Like *me*," she said. "We could have a lot of fun together if you'd just get real."

"What kind of fun?" I said, flopping down on my bed. "I thought you didn't believe in fun."

"Oh, so your idea of fun is sex, is that it?" Molly asked. She sighed loudly, like she was sick of me already. "Is there like, a law or something that says we have to fight about sex at least once every time we talk?"

"I just think it's weird that if you like me so much you're not even thinking of us doing it. Doesn't that seem weird to you?"

"No. You know what that's called?" Molly said impatiently. "It's called common sense. You know what happens if we sleep together? You dump me."

"How can I dump you if we haven't even started going out yet?" I asked, frustrated. I

———■———

scraped at the place on my pillow where Honey had drawn the X. It didn't look like it was going to come out.

"Jonah, we're not having sex, okay? At least not yet," she qualified.

"Whoa," I said. "So that means there's a chance it might actually happen?"

"Maybe," Molly said. "First we have to find out if we're compatible."

"How do we do that?"

She giggled. "You'll see."

I think this was supposed to be funny, but something about it really annoyed me. Molly can be so full of herself. And she seems to get off on toying with me. I hate it.

"Uh-oh. Now you're mad," she said.

"I didn't say anything!" I said, picking up my pillow and throwing it across my room. It bounced off the sliding glass doors that lead to the pool. Honey was out there, tanning herself in her black bathing suit. She's been trying to get a tan for weeks, but she's still really pale.

"Well, if you weren't mad, you would say something," Molly insisted. "I think you're mad."

"Whatever," I said.

"Fine," she said back.

All of a sudden I was really tired of talking to

—■—

her. All she does is play games. But then she said something that made me laugh.

"So, what are you wearing?" she asked, out of the blue.

"You're crazy," I told her.

"Exactly," she said.

Jan. 13

I went down to the Dune after school today, just to look at the ocean and try to think some things over. When we were in ninth grade, the Dune was the coolest place to hang out in Pompano, but when I came back this fall it was different. Nobody really goes there anymore. It's weird.

Before I went there, I walked down to the lifeguard tower to see if Pops Berman was around, but he wasn't. I sat in the tower and looked out at the ocean. In the distance, some people were flying radio-controlled airplanes. It was kind of cool to watch the planes doing these dives and circling around each other.

They made this high-pitched whining sound and started to have kind of a dogfight. I decided to walk up the beach and get a better look.

As I got closer I was surprised to find that the two people flying the planes were girls, wearing bikinis. One was this dark-skinned muscular girl I'd never seen before. The other was Posie. I didn't know she was into planes, but I am no longer surprised by anything Posie does. She's sort of changed since she started going out with Lamar Jameson and hanging out with all the kids from Ely High. She's like, more aloof and confident.

There's nothing geekier than flying remote-controlled airplanes, but of course Posie made it look like the coolest thing in the world. She was wearing these mirrored sunglasses and the bikini she had on was bright, bright orange. Her fingernails and toenails were painted silver. She was chewing gum with her mouth kind of open and her face was lit up with this electric smile as she watched her plane.

Suddenly, one of the planes sort of sputtered and died and went into a tailspin. A moment later it crashed on the beach, and its wings broke off.

The other girl just sort of stood there staring at it for a moment. It was her plane. Posie's plane buzzed over the site of the crash and waggled its wings. The other girl walked over and picked up the pieces of her plane and started walking away. Posie

---

shouted something after her, but I couldn't quite hear what she'd said.

"Hey, Posie," I called. "What's up?"

"Hey," Posie said. "You're Jonah Black! Didn't we used to be friends or something?"

She glanced at me for a second, then returned her gaze to the sky. She held a radio-control unit in her hands, with a long antenna that she kept pointed at the moving biplane.

"Since when were you into planes?" I asked.

Posie didn't answer. She just kept on flying her plane.

My eyes fell upon the place at the bottom of Posie's throat, where her collarbones met. I remembered kissing that exact place when we were going out. Then I remembered the night that we were about to sleep together and I called her Sophie by accident. It was the worst thing I've ever done. But Posie forgave me. She's incredible.

"Hey, Jonah," she said. "Hold this for a second, 'kay?" She handed me the remote control and then she ran toward the ocean and dove under the waves. I just stood there watching her in the water. There is nothing more perfect than Posie in the surf. She went under for a second, then she surfaced and started doing a strong breaststroke against the current.

The tide was going out, leaving conches and clams on the beach. Foam sizzled on the white sand.

The sound of an engine drew nearer, and I realized I was holding the remote control without even looking at where the plane was. It was buzzing straight toward me, and I had no idea how to fly the thing.

I pushed the biggest lever up, assuming that would make the plane go up again. Instead, it went into a plunging nosedive. Posie's plane was about to smash straight into the sand.

Then Posie appeared out of nowhere, dripping wet, and grabbed the remote control out of my hands. She pushed some levers and the plane started climbing again.

"Jesus, Jonah. Remind me never to get in a plane with you, okay?" she joked.

"Sorry," I said. Posie was piloting the plane now. Water was running down her back. Each drop captured the sunlight and sparkled against her tan skin.

"Who was that you were with before? The girl whose plane crashed?" I asked.

"Oh, her," Posie said. "That's Kassandra. Lamar's ex-girlfriend. She thought she could get in my face with that pathetic Sopwith Camel. I just had to shoot her down!"

Posie spat out her gum with a sound like *phooo.*

"A Sopwith Camel? What's that?" I asked.

"World War One biplane. You know, Snoopy flies one in the *Peanuts* comics."

I just looked at her, amazed.

"Oh, come on, Jonah. Like you never read the comics." Posie laughed.

"Actually, I'm usually too busy doing intellectual stuff, like reading encyclopedias and studying for my SATs," I joked.

"Yeah, right," Posie said, laughing. Her teeth flashed white in the sunshine. "You mean you're too busy chasing girls around."

"What's wrong with that?" I said. I liked it that she thought I was this big stud.

"So what's up, Jonah?" she said. "I never see you anymore. Did you ever figure out what to do about what's-her-face? The psycho chick?"

"Sophie," I said. "She's in some hospital now. I am *so* over her." I tried to sound nonchalant. Posie smiled at me.

"What's so funny?" I said.

"Listen to you. 'I am so over her.' You think I'm gonna fall for that?"

I shrugged. "I don't know. I guess I just want to be over her, that's all."

The plane did a loop-de-loop.

* * *

"Thorne says you're going out with some chick from St. Winnifred's," Posie said.

"Yeah. Molly Beale," I said.

"Never heard of her," said Posie. "She doesn't surf, does she?"

"Nope." To be honest, I felt kind of embarrassed talking to Posie about another girl. I mean, the original deal was, we broke up so I could get my head straight about Sophie. And here I was, talking to her about Molly, and my head was still not straight about Sophie. And Molly and I weren't even really going out yet, but I didn't tell her that.

There are some days when I wish I could trade both of them to get Posie back. But I already had my chance to have Posie, and I messed it up, badly.

"So what's she like?" Posie asked.

"I don't know," I said. "She's really smart. She's funny. She's a terrible driver."

"Yeah, well, you want to know what sucks, Jonah?" Posie asked me.

"What?"

"Me having to find out you're going out with somebody from Thorne. Why don't you call me anymore? I used to be your best friend."

"I know," I said. "It's been . . . I don't know. Weird."

—— ■ ——

Posie looked at me. "Does she know you're still all mental about Sophie?"

I didn't answer right away. Posie buzzed me with her plane and I ducked to avoid getting beheaded.

"Hey, I don't know," I said, annoyed. "Do I have to tell everyone everything?"

Posie put her arm around my shoulder and squeezed it. "It's okay," she said. "There's really nothing wrong with being mental."

At that moment this huge, radio-controlled stealth plane came buzzing down out of the sky. It soared above us.

"Hey!" Posie said, all excited. "It's Lamar!"

I turned around and saw Lamar Jameson, who is about the hugest guy I know, standing on top of a dune behind us. Posie took her arm off of my shoulder and waved. I thought about the times Lamar and I had competed against each other in diving meets. Since I broke my arm, Don Shula High's team has gone completely to hell. Ely High is now number one in Broward County. Thanks to Lamar.

"I'd better be going," I said.

"No, wait," Posie said. "Stay. I want you and Lamar to be friends."

The stealth plane descended straight toward me. It dove faster and faster. I ducked and covered my face with my arms.

At the last second, the plane pulled up. Lamar came down from the dune grinning this huge grin.

"Hey, Sweetie," Posie said, and gave him this huge wet kiss. It was funny to see the two of them making out, while holding their remote-control units behind each others' backs.

Then Lamar looked over at me and nodded. "Hey, Jonah," he said. "How's the arm?"

I was wishing Northgirl hadn't written MARRY ME, JONAH on the side of the cast. It's pretty embarrassing.

"It's okay," I said. "How's diving?"

"It's okay, man," said Lamar, trying to be modest.

"So who do you think you're going against in the finals?" I asked. It was either Ft. Lauderdale or Tampa.

"Tampa, definitely," Lamar said. He looked up at his plane. "Definitely Tampa."

"I'm so glad you guys are hitting it off!" Posie said. It was funny, until that moment we almost were hitting it off. But as soon as she said that I felt self-conscious, like we were being forced to talk to each other. I mean, Lamar's not stupid. He knew I'd gone out with Posie—even if it was only for like, five minutes. And he knew that Posie and I have been friends since grade school. If I were him, I wouldn't have wanted me around.

"Well, okay then," I said. It was time to go.

"Okay," said Lamar.

—■—

"See you guys," I said and started walking away.

"Hey, listen, Jonah," Lamar started to say.

I stopped walking and looked at him. He was even huger up close than he'd seemed at the end of the diving board.

"You're good, you know?" Lamar told me.

It took me a second to figure out what he meant. He meant I was a good diver.

"Thanks," I said. "So are you."

"No," he said. "I meant it. You're—well, yeah. Good."

I nodded. It was a pretty cool thing for him to say. And he was being honest about it. He didn't say I was great, because I'm not. *He's* great. He's like, the best diver I've ever seen. Anyway, him saying that made me feel like Posie is in good hands. I think Lamar is a pretty decent guy.

"I'll catch up with you later," I told Posie.

"Okay, see ya, Jonah," she said, looking up at her plane. I walked away down the beach. From behind me I heard the sound of two planes, circling each other.

Jan. 14, 10 P.M.

I had a feeling Molly was going to call me, and I really didn't feel like talking to her, so I logged on to talk to Northgirl so the line would be busy. Molly never calls after ten because she thinks it's rude. I guess she's just trying to be polite, but no one in this house goes to bed before midnight anyway.

AMERICA ONLINE
INSTANT MESSAGE FROM NORTHGIRL999,
1-14, 9:41 P.M.

NORTHGIRL999: Hi, Jonah!

JBLACK94710: Hey, Northgirl. How have you been?

NORTHGIRL999: I'm all right. I think I have a new boyfriend.

JBLACK94710: I'm sorry to hear that. I thought you were waiting for me.

———■———

NORTHGIRL999: I am waiting for you, you bonehead. When you figure out who I am, I'll drop this guy and start things up with you that minute. Deal?

JBLACK94710: Okay. Can you give me any new clues about who you are?

NORTHGIRL999: I don't think so.

JBLACK94710: Come on, just one? It's driving me crazy!

NORTHGIRL999: I'm glad it's driving you crazy. Now you know how I feel, sort of.

JBLACK94710: You won't even give me a hint?

NORTHGIRL999: Well, tell me what you know.

JBLACK94710: What do I know about you? Well, you say you're somebody I see all the time.

NORTHGIRL999: Right.

JBLACK94710: And you know practically everything about me.

NORTHGIRL999: Yup.

JBLACK94710: And you're a girl. You PROMISE me you're a girl, right? I mean, you're not like Mr. Bond or something?

NORTHGIRL999: You mean, Robere?

JBLACK94710: See, look at that—you even know Mr. Bond's stupid first name.

NORTHGIRL999: Jonah, everybody at Don Shula knows Mr. Bond's stupid first name.

JBLACK94710: WAIT. YOU GO TO DON SHULA???

NORTHGIRL999: Of course.

JBLACK94710: You never told me that before. That is a huge hint.

NORTHGIRL999: Okay, so who am I?

———■———

JBLACK94710: Um. Well, first let me decide who you're not. You're NOT Posie Hoff.

NORTHGIRL999: I am definitely not Posie. Puh-lease.

JBLACK94710: And you're not Kirsten, or Cilla, or Cecily.

NORTHGIRL999: Cold, colder, coldest.

JBLACK94710: And you promise me you're not my sister, Honey?

NORTHGIRL999: Eww, gross!

JBLACK94710: But you're somebody I see all the time.

NORTHGIRL999: Yeah, somebody you totally IGNORE.

JBLACK94710: Um . . .

NORTHGIRL999: Somebody who thinks you're totally HOT. Somebody who would do it with you in FIVE SECONDS if you asked. Somebody who thinks about what you look like with your clothes off, all the time. Somebody who goes to all your diving matches just so I can see your pecs.

JBLACK94710: Can I ask you a question?

NORTHGIRL999: You can ask me anything you like, Mr. Wooden Head.

JBLACK94710: When I finally meet you, how am I going to know it's you?

NORTHGIRL999: You will, Jonah. I promise, you will.

Jan. 16

When I got home from school today, there was a package waiting for me. It was postmarked Bryn Mawr, Pennsylvania, and at first I thought it was from Dad. But then I realized the handwriting wasn't his—it was Sophie's! On the outside of the box it said PRECIOUS AND FRAGILE, which are the words I'd use to describe her, if I had to.

I took the box into my room and opened it up. There were lots and lots of rolled-up newspapers protecting whatever it was. The newspapers were all *Philadelphia Inquirers*. I didn't even know they were allowed to read newspapers in Maggins.

I kept pulling out the balls of newspaper and unwrapping each one. They were all empty. I started thinking, well, it wouldn't really surprise me

—■—

if Sophie sent me a present that contains nothing.

Finally I unwrapped a big ball at the bottom of the box, and inside it was a small Ziploc bag. And inside that was a dead hummingbird. There wasn't a note or anything.

I sat there for a moment holding the bird in the plastic bag, just looking at it. Then I got angry. This whole time I'd been hoping that there was some sort of gift inside the box that would acknowledge what I'd done for her; the connection that we have. I was hoping she'd sent me—I don't know—a ring, or an arrowhead, or a stone from the beach in front of her house in Maine, or a horseshoe from one of her horses. Even a nice long letter from her would have been good. In fact, that would have been best of all. It was about time Sophie wrote me a nice long letter explaining why she cried every time we were about to have sex, or why she painted that picture of herself about to jump off a cliff. That explained . . . I don't know. That would explain *her.* Instead, I got this. A dead bird. I guess she really is nuts.

I looked at one of the pieces of newspaper. It was the horoscope page. One of the listings, for Gemini, was circled. *You will find yourself pulled in many directions. Avoid making any decisions now.* I've never really believed in astrology, and I'm not a

———■———

Gemini, I'm a Cancer, but the horoscope seemed to describe exactly how I feel about Sophie.

Then I got scared. I'd been so wrapped up in thinking about how mad I was, that I hadn't even thought about Sophie. She's reached the point in her life where she is sending people dead hummingbirds? What the hell is wrong with her???

I wanted to call Sophie on the phone, tell her I love her, ask her if she's okay. But the more I thought about it, the more I was like, whoa. She sends you a dead hummingbird and you're wondering if she's okay? I think this is a question I already know the answer to.

What I can't stop thinking about is how Honey is going up there, to Pennsylvania. I could go with her. I could go see Sophie.

AMERICA ONLINE MAIL

To: BetsD8@MastheadAcademy.edu
From: JBlack94710@aol.com

Hey, Betsy. I'm sorry I didn't write you back when you wrote me before. That was like, December, I guess. I appreciate you trying to warn me about Sophie. Maybe you know she and I got together between Christmas and New Year's. She came down to Florida with her family and the two of us met

---

in a hotel in Orlando. It was all pretty weird, actually. She kind of freaked out on me and ran off. This was in Disney World. Then I got a letter from her a week or two later and she told me she's in Maggins now. It was this really sad letter, and she was begging me to come rescue her. Since then I haven't heard from her, except yesterday I got a package from her in the mail—she sent me a dead bird. It's kind of giving me the creeps.

The weird thing is that I still think about her all the time. Do you think that means I'm crazy? Did you ever have that feeling, like you couldn't stop thinking about someone, even though you knew you shouldn't?

I guess I feel sorry for her. I feel like maybe in some bizarre way I'm the only person she trusts.

Well, anyway . . . How is everything at Masthead? You must be waiting to find out where you got in to college. Where do you want to go? My sister, Honey, is already in at Harvard. She's going up there in a few days to visit the campus and meet some professors and I guess do whatever she can to make sure everyone there regrets they ever let her in. :) (This would make a lot more sense to you if you ever met my sister, who is pretty strange.)

Anyway, I also wanted to say that I'm glad you tried to stay in touch with me, even though I didn't write you back right away. I feel bad. You were really nice to me when I was at Masthead, and I always kind of wish we'd gotten to know each other better. I'm sorry if I let you down or anything. You're a great girl, Betsy. If I could do Masthead all over again, I wouldn't spend all my time obsessed with Sophie!!! Well, you know what I mean. I hope so, anyway. And I hope you aren't offended by any of this. You're just a cool girl, and I should have told you last year when I was around. Thanks for looking out for me.

Maybe we could talk on the phone sometime.

Jonah

—■—

Jan. 17, 4:30 P.M.

I'm lying in my room eating Cocoa Puffs out of the box, which makes me feel like I'm about six years old. Honey is going through this whole Cocoa Puffs phase right now; it's all she eats—three meals a day. Mom says she isn't worried. She says that sugar is "our way of saying hello to our own energy." Honey fills her cheeks with them so she looks like a hamster, then she pushes her palms against her cheeks and crushes the Cocoa Puffs against her teeth. Then she washes them down with Coke. Last night I watched her doing this, and she said, "You should try some, Octopus Face. They make everything taste like a frigging chocolate milk shake."

Anyway, Thorne and I hung out after school today. It was just like old times. We went down to

———■———

the Dune. Thorne was smoking clove cigarettes. He said they were imported from India. Man, if I lived in India and there were cigarettes like this there, I'd want to send them out of the country, too. They smell like a perfumed, dead animal. I told Thorne that and he said I just didn't appreciate the finer things.

"If the finer things smell like roadkill," I said, "I think I can skip them."

"Jonah, dude," said Thorne, taking a big suck on his clove cigarette and sending the smoke rings sailing out toward the ocean. "You're not thinking positively."

"What's positive about nasty cigarettes?" I said.

"Chicks love them," he said.

"Yeah," I said, "but they probably give you worse cancer than regular cigarettes."

Thorne just shook his head. "You don't get cancer when you're eighteen," he said.

Stupidity of this kind pisses me off, but I decided not to bother getting mad at him. If you want to be friends with Thorne, you just sort of take him as a package. So I just kicked at the sand and didn't say anything.

"So what's up with you and that girl Molly?" Thorne said. "Elanor Brubaker says she's a couple astronauts short of a shuttle mission."

"Elanor's wrong," I said. "She's a genius."

Thorne shook his head. "Just because she's a genius doesn't mean she isn't stupid, dude. Hell, look at your sister. A prime example of what I call Negative Intelligence."

"Negative Intelligence?" I said. I knew I was about to hear one of Thorne's stupid, made-up theories. I don't think Thorne even believes what he says half the time. But he says it anyway.

"Yeah, yeah," he said. "You see, Jonahman, there's two kinds of smart: There's smart-smart and there's stupid-smart. Smart-smart is like Einstein or Thomas Edison. Then there's stupid-smart. Like your sister, Honey, or Molly Beale, or, say, Bill Clinton. Man, there's a prime example. You score a million points on your SAT, but you can't take a dump without it landing on your foot. In fact, for a lot of people, the more they study, the dumber they get. It's like in school, where you go into a class thinking you understand something, and an hour later you leave the room and you realize you don't have a clue. You actually leave the class stupider than you went in. I think most people's intelligence peaks at age fourteen. From there, it's all downhill."

I smiled. "So what makes people stupid?"

"Education, man," said Thorne, stubbing out his cigarette in the sand and leaning back on his elbows. He surveyed the sea. "Education is the number one cause of stupidity."

"So what does this have to do with Molly?" I said.

Thorne reached into his backpack and got the package of clove cigarettes and shook another one out. "She's a textbook case," he said, lighting up.

"How do you know?"

"'Cause you immediately said she was smart, which means her smartness is getting in the way of everything else. Like, you didn't say she has a great ass, or she kisses like a professional," Thorne said.

I rolled my eyes. "You're not really smoking another one of those fart cigarettes, are you?"

"Why, you want one?" he said.

"No, thanks."

"Come on, dude." Thorne stuck one in my mouth and lit it. It was awful, and I hadn't even inhaled it. "You can't get into college unless you can smoke these," he said.

"Is that right?" I said. "Maybe I'll just join the army."

"You gotta smoke there, too. For pretty much anything you do, you have to know how to smoke."

I held the cigarette and watched the ocean. The wind was blowing Thorne's hair around. I hated to admit it, but with the clove cigarette in one hand, he really did look like the world's coolest dude. Until you smelled him, anyway.

I took a puff on the clove cigarette and started coughing. It felt like someone had pointed a blow-torch at my lungs.

"Suave, Jonah," Thorne said. "Real suave."

"Shut up." I coughed again.

"Hey, I told my Dad you're ready to start working on the *Scrod*," Thorne said. "Now that you aren't working at First Amendment anymore."

"I told you before, I'm not working on the *Scrod*, okay?" I said. "I don't want to clean fish with your dad."

"You and me both," Thorne said, and for just a second, he kind of dropped his whole cool-dude routine. I thought about how crummy his house was, and how Thorne hustled and schemed to make extra cash. I felt bad.

"Anyway, who says I'm not working at First Amendment anymore?" I said.

"You don't have a bicycle, do you? Since Molly the Genius ran over it with her car?" he said.

"No."

"And you've failed your driving test, uh—how many times now?" Thorne reminded me.

I didn't answer.

———■———

"Uh-huh. So how are you delivering pizzas and videos again?"

"I'm going to get another bike," I told him.

"Okay," said Thorne. "But you don't even need a bike to work for my Dad."

"Thorne," I said. "Forget it."

"Okay. Whatever," said Thorne.

He lay on his back and blew smoke up into the air. I stubbed my cigarette out and buried it deep in the sand. My mouth tasted awful. I don't think I'll ever eat enough Cocoa Puffs to get rid of that taste.

"Hey, Jonah," said Thorne. "After you break up with Molly? You think I could try her out?"

I couldn't believe he'd said that. He wasn't kidding, either. He made it sound like Molly was a car he wanted to test-drive or something.

"I'm not breaking up with her, all right?" I said, defensively.

"Okay," Thorne said.

"I thought you said she was stupid-smart, anyway."

"I did," Thorne said. "But I know how to fix that."

"How?"

"A week of intense one-on-one instruction with the esteemed Thorne Wood, and you know what happens?" he said.

"What?" I asked, although I didn't really care what the answer was.

"She gets stupid-stupid."

"And that's good?" I said.

Thorne lifted his head and grinned at me. "That's *real* good," he said.

I had to laugh, I couldn't help it. Thorne cracks me up.

Jan. 18

Awesome news!!! The cast came off today. The doctor who was checking it said it had healed nicely. Now I have to do these exercises to strengthen my arm. It feels kind of numb and weak, but it's definitely good to have the cast off.

Anyway, the way he removed it was kind of funny. The doctor had this little saw that went right through the plaster. It was scary, like some kind of horror movie where he was going to cut my arm off. He sawed right down the middle where it says MARRY ME, JONAH, and the cast broke into two big pieces. The air was filled with plaster dust. It was cool.

I got to take the pieces home, and now they're sitting on top of my dresser.

I'm supposed to do these little bicep curls while holding a small can of niblet corn. Once I get good at that I'm supposed to use a can of peaches. Then a large can of crushed tomatoes. I've got all the cans lined up on my desk.

Too bad I've missed the rest of diving season, which totally sucks. The thing that drives me crazy most of all is that we have one last meet against Ely High this weekend, and I would have loved to compete against Lamar Jameson one last time and smoked his ass on the high board. It would have been nice for Posie to see me do that.

Jan. 23, 9:30 P.M.

Today was the swim meet against Ely, which I watched from the bleachers with Posie, Caitlin (her little sister), and Thorne. Ely totally wasted us! I'd like to say that this was partly because I wasn't out there diving for the team, but even if I'd been there, it wouldn't have been enough to turn it around. The Ely guys have definitely been practicing. And Lamar is better than ever. It's like his muscles have muscles. It's sick.

Posie watched Lamar do this one dive, and she didn't say anything. He did a triple somersault in reverse, absolutely perfectly. Posie just sat there and watched him do the dive, and afterward Kassandra—who was sitting with the Ely fans—started squealing and shouting, "You got it, baby!"

Lamar surfaced and looked at her and smiled, and the next thing I knew, Posie was up and on her way out of the stands.

I turned to Thorne and Caitlin and found that they were kissing, and I don't mean just kissing, I mean they were like, *spelunking* in each other's mouths. I wondered if maybe it was a mirage that was going to vanish and I was just imagining the whole thing. But no, Caitlin Hoff and Thorne were seriously going at it. I couldn't believe it.

I kind of have a bad attitude about Posie's little sister anyway, because she always acts like she hates me and she thinks I'm stupid-stupid. But I was also pretty annoyed that Thorne hadn't said anything about Caitlin the other day when the two of us were sitting on the sand dune smoking those fart cigarettes and talking about Molly. I guess sometimes I get tired of the way Thorne never really talks to me about stuff. I mean, are he and Caitlin a big secret? It didn't look like it. Then I realized maybe one reason he hadn't said anything is he didn't even know he was going to hook up with her. I mean, he may not have known he was going to hook up with Caitlin Hoff until five minutes after he'd already started doing it.

Anyway, I kind of cleared my throat, and they came up for air. Thorne looked at me and said with

—■—

this big shit-eating grin, "Whoa, Caitie. Don't look now but Jonah's just figured something out."

Caitlin kind of glared at me. She looks a lot like Posie, but she definitely doesn't act like her. Posie got all the sun and she got all the rain. "Jonah who?" she said, in this kind of bored way.

"Posie just left, in case you guys didn't notice," I said. "She looked upset."

"Duh," said Caitlin. It was such a tenth-grade thing to say. She kind of flicked her hair behind her ear in this snooty-bitch way and I looked at Thorne as if to say, *Dude, what are you thinking?*

"Well, Jonah?" Caitlin said. "Aren't you going to go running after her, like you always do?"

She said it like doing this was an incredibly stupid idea, but then she said, "Oh, never mind. I'll do it." She got up and headed out in the same direction Posie had gone. I guess going after Posie was only a stupid idea if *I* did it.

The competition was almost over. There were only two more sucky Don Shula divers left. I couldn't even bear to watch.

"You know what, Thorne," I said. "I don't think your girlfriend likes me."

"Yeah. To be honest," Thorne said, "she hates you, dude."

I think maybe I'd had two conversations with

—■—

Caitlin in my life. "Why does she hate me?" I asked.

Thorne yawned. "She thinks you screwed with Posie's head."

"Oh, and you didn't?" I challenged.

"Not like you did," Thorne said.

"So what's up with you and her, anyway? You couldn't find anybody who wasn't in elementary school?"

"Believe me, she's mature for her age," Thorne said.

"Yeah," I said. "Unlike you."

At that second I saw the girl who I'd only seen before from the high dive, the girl I always call Watches Boys Dive because she looks American Indian and comes to all the diving meets. I even thought she might be Northgirl. She was sitting all the way across the bleachers, but I had never been this close to her before.

I almost told Thorne, but then I had this thought, like Watches Boys Dive is *mine*. I didn't want him to even know about her. So I just got up and went out to the aisle and walked five steps up to her level, and then I started saying *excuse me* to everybody, trying to get to where she was sitting. There was even a free spot on the bench next to her and I thought, *Yes, I am finally going to meet her!*

■

Suddenly she looked up at me, and there was a look of total panic on her face. She leaped to her feet and grabbed her bag and almost stepped on about twelve people in her hurry to get out of there. Then she ran down the steps on the other side of the bleachers. I said "excuse me" some more, and I got to the aisle and started running after her. When I got out in the hallway, I could hear the echoing sound of everybody applauding and cheering after somebody's dive. Way ahead of me was Watches Boys Dive, running around a corner. Her bag was trailing behind her like the tail on a kite. I ran after her and followed her outside.

Suddenly her bag fell onto the blacktop and all the stuff inside it spilled out. I started walking toward her while she was on her knees, picking up stuff. When she heard me, she got up and started to run off across the parking lot.

"Wait!" I yelled at her. "I have to talk to you!"

I ran after her, but soon I was standing on the highway, with the Intercoastal Waterway across the street and no sign of her anywhere. It was kind of creepy. She had totally vanished!

The mystery was not solved. If anything, it had become more confusing than ever.

I walked back toward Don Shula High and there in the middle of the parking lot, right where she'd

—■—

dropped her bag, were three things she hadn't picked up. The first was a tube of lipstick—the color was called Baby Kiss. It looked like one of those lipsticks girls use to make it look like they're not wearing any lipstick. Sophie always wears those.

The second was a pack of matches from something called The Fur Room. Underneath that it said POMPANO BEACH, but I'd never heard of a bar called The Fur Room in Pompano before. It sounded pretty sketchy. There was no address.

And the third thing was a picture of me. It was the photo that had appeared in the school paper back at the beginning of the diving season. It looked like she'd carried it around in her purse for a long time. Yikes.

—■—

Jan. 24, 5:30 P.M.

It's after school and I'm sitting here looking at this huge pile of homework and I'm just not in the mood. German sucks.

Sophie sent me another letter today. Here it is:

Dear Jonah,

Sorry about the hummingbird. You probably think I'm completely insane. But I found it during "outside time" yesterday, this poor little dead bird, and I thought, this is me, *and then I thought,* you know, Jonah is the only person who would understand what I mean. *So I sent it to you, but now you must think I'm totally sick.*

I've been reading this book about Amelia

Earhart. You know who she is, right? She was this pilot in the 1920s and she was trying to become the first woman to circle the globe in a plane. Supposedly her plane crashed in the Pacific Ocean, but they never found the wreck, and some people think maybe her plane didn't really crash at all. I was thinking if I ever get out of here, I'd like to travel to the islands in the Pacific Ocean and try to find her. If she's alive now, she'd be like 95 years old or something, but maybe she'd tell her story if you asked her in the right way. Doesn't that sound possible, that she just pretended to disappear, then lived on some island for 80 years drinking coconut milk and weaving palm leaves?

Anyway, sorry if I weirded you out with the bird. I'm doing better, I think, but I'm lonely. Sometimes I think I'm the loneliest girl in the world. I guess Amelia must be pretty lonely, too.

Love,
Sophie

What's funny is that this letter did get through to me, in a way. I mean, what she said about the bird and everything. I do know what she means.

I don't know much about Amelia Earhart, but I asked Mom and she got all excited, telling me what a great heroine she was.

"She was so brave!" Mom said, her eyes tearing up.

Later, Posie called me and I asked her about Amelia Earhart.

"She was like, the first woman to rock the globe, you know what I mean?" Posie said breathlessly. "Sometimes when I surf I think about her. I think about how I want to just keep going. But I always wind up back on the beach. Amelia—she just kept going."

I can't believe all these women think Amelia Earhart is so incredibly important. Neither Mom nor Posie could tell me the name of the woman who actually *did* first circle the globe successfully in a plane—but they all knew the story about Amelia Earhart like she was their own grandmother.

I called Thorne later and asked him if he knew anything about her, and of course he didn't have a clue.

"Amelia Earhart?" he said. I could hear him, thinking hard. "She go to St. Winnifred's? What's she look like?"

Anyway, now I can't stop thinking about Amelia

Earhart. Mom even has a book about her, and there's pictures of her in it. She was actually pretty cute. But the thing that interests me most about her is what a hero she is, even though she actually died trying to do the thing she set out to do. I mean, she never actually achieved her goal, but that isn't what mattered. I guess the lesson of Amelia Earhart is that it's not the getting there that's important, it's the journey, and having the guts to set off on the journey in the first place.

Maybe I should go up to Pennsylvania with Honey after all. Even if it ends in disaster.

—■—

Jan. 25

I've been canceling my appointments, but I finally met with Dr. LaRue today. I'm still mad at him from when I called him from Orlando and heard him peeing while he was talking to me. I don't know why this bothered me so much, but it just seems like he could have excused himself. I wasn't going anywhere. And it's not just that he was peeing, but that he thought I'd be dumb enough not to recognize the sound of him peeing when I heard it coming over the phone. He even flushed, which is a pretty unmistakable sound. I think my shrink needs to learn how to be more sensitive to people's feelings.

Actually the big news is that Dr. LaRue has shaved off his mustache! He no longer looks like

—— ■ ——

one of the Muppets. In fact, he looks a lot younger and better looking.

“Hey, you look great, Doc,” I said, when I sat down in the big armchair across from his desk.

His hand went to his face. He rubbed his upper lip and smiled, like he was embarrassed that I’d noticed and pleased at the same time. “Why, thank you, Jonah,” he said.

I noticed there was also a new plant in his office. This giant cactus. It seemed like the worst idea in the world, to put a cactus in a room where people are trying to tell you about their problems. Cactuses aren’t exactly soothing.

Anyway, today he wanted to know all about Sophie and Molly, and I told him that I like Molly but I don’t like the way she teases me. Like, how she brings up sex just so she can remind me that she doesn’t want to do it.

“And you think sex is important?” Dr. LaRue said. “Important to your relationship with Molly, I mean.”

"Well, yeah,” I said, as if this was the dumbest question in the world. “She claims to have done it lots of times before, so why can’t we do it?”

“Do you think you will be able to keep going out with Molly if she won’t sleep with you?” Dr. LaRue asked.

—■—

"We're not even really going out yet! All we do is talk about what it's going to be like once we are going out, and we get into these stupid fights where I feel like I'm this bad dog who's peed on the rug. But she's the one who started it."

"Is it that you feel that Molly doesn't think you're worthy? Do you feel put down, Jonah?"

"I don't know. Maybe," I said. I hadn't really thought of it that way. That's the thing about therapy. You can think about things in ways you wouldn't normally, but sometimes it can feel like words are being put into your mouth. It's kind of unnerving.

Dr. LaRue fingered his upper lip, except now there wasn't any mustache to finger.

"And how does Sophie make you feel? Does she make you feel the same way?" he asked.

"No."

"How does Sophie make you feel?" he repeated.

I looked over at the cactus. It looked prickly.

"She admires me," I said. "She says I'm her hero."

From outside I could hear the sound of an airplane flying overhead, probably making a landing at the Pompano Airport. I wondered if the blimp was back yet.

"Is that why she's important to you?" Dr. LaRue asked me.

—■—

"Maybe," I said, annoyed that he'd made me admit this. "It's nice when someone thinks of you that way."

"But is that a good reason to pursue a relationship with her?" he said. "Is that a good reason to jeopardize your relationship with Molly?"

"Probably not," I said. "No."

Dr. LaRue smiled. "Very good, Jonah," he said. "You're learning, aren't you?"

I thought this was sort of a condescending thing to say, but then he stood up and added, "Will you excuse me just a second? I have to go to the men's room." And then he left the room.

At least he didn't make me listen to it that time. Maybe Dr. LaRue is learning something, too.

—■—

Jan. 26

Today I went over to First Amendment Pizza to talk to Mr. Swede. When I first told him my bike got crushed, Mr. Swede said not to worry, he'd hold my job until I could buy a new bicycle. I haven't really been in any hurry to get one, though, because what I really want is to get my driver's license so I won't need a bike anymore, and if I go out and buy a new bike it's sort of like admitting I'm never going to pass the test. I haven't even scheduled another one yet. I guess I'm scared of flunking it again.

To be honest, I kind of hate delivering pizzas and videos anyway. So the little vacation from my job was totally fine with me.

Anyway, Mr. Swede called while I was out yesterday and he told Mom that he wanted to see me. So

---

I went over there because I figured he wanted to give me the money he owes me. Which he did. He handed me the envelope with $72.75 in it. And then he fired me.

"Yonah, you buy new bicycle?" he said. He came out from behind the counter and was wiping his head with a big white cloth.

"Not yet," I said.

"Are you going to buy bicycle? Tell the truth!"

Mr. Swede is always really sweaty. He kept dabbing at his sweaty head with this marinara-stained cloth. If I was hungry and went into First Amendment for some pizza, just looking at Mr. Swede would take away my appetite.

"I keep meaning to," I said, but it was a lie. I didn't ever want another bicycle. I wanted a Ford Focus, or better yet, a BMW.

"Yonah, I have boy with car, wants job. Dooba cannot deliver all by self. Pizzas get cold! Customers mad!" He smacked his hand on the countertop, which kind of scared me. I'd never seen Mr. Swede so mad.

Doober, the other delivery guy, was sitting at one of the booths, smoking a Camel. I think the reason the pizzas were cold was that Doober was sitting there smoking instead of putting them in his Toyota pickup and making the deliveries. But if I said

—— ■ ——

something, Doober would just look pissed off and say, "Hey, man. I'm on a break." Doober is always on a break.

"Yonah, I need delivery boy. Now, is he named Yonah?"

"I just need to buy a bike, Mr. Swede. I'll get around to it, I promise. Things have been pretty crazy for me lately," I told him.

"I call boy with car. You, Yonah. You finished."

I realized I was getting fired.

"I'll go out and get a bike tomorrow, if you need me to—" I told him.

That was kind of a weird thing to say since I didn't really want to work at First Amendment anymore. But I hated being fired. I wanted to quit. Getting fired made me feel like a total loser.

"Good-bye, Yonah!"

Mr. Swede opened the door and I walked through it. I was sort of in a daze, like I had nowhere to go. I felt disconnected from everything. As I was walking, this girl stopped me on the street and asked me for the time. I hadn't even seen her until the second she opened her mouth, that's how spaced out I was. The girl was small and blond and thin and she was wearing a black tank top, a black denim miniskirt, and a strange leather hat on her head.

"What?" I said, startled.

—■—

"The time?" she said and smiled at me.

"The time," I said. "Right, the time."

"Jonah," Sophie says, pulling the flaps of her hat down over her ears and buckling it under her chin. It's an aviator's cap, and she's wearing a bomber jacket, too. The wind is blowing her hair around. "It's me."

"Sophie," I say. "I didn't even recognize you!"

She just shakes her head and smiles like I'm kind of stupid, and I wonder, am I stupid-stupid, or am I smart-stupid? Then I remember that she wants to know what time it is so I look at my watch. The hands are frozen at four o'clock. There are even little icicles hanging from the hour hand.

"I think it's four," I say, shivering in my T-shirt. It's really getting cold now. "But my watch is broken."

"I don't mind," she says. "Four o'clock." She thinks this over. A big strong gust of wind blows in from the ocean, and her hair streams out behind her. "That still leaves us lots of time."

"Time for what?" I say.

"Time to fly, Jonah," she says, and leads me across the runway to this big old plane. It has two big propellers and on the side of the plane it says LOCKHEED ELECTRA. Sophie climbs on board, and a white scarf flutters around her neck in the harsh

—■—

wind. Suddenly I get a very bad feeling. Something in me says, *Do not get on this plane.*

Sophie puts her hand out to me. "Come on," she says. "Don't you want to fly?"

It is a very hard question to answer.

"What's so hard about it?" the blond girl said. She pointed at my watch. "Why don't you just look at your watch?"

"Oh, yeah," I said, completely embarrassed. I wondered how long I had stood there, staring at her like an idiot. I looked at my watch. It was working fine. "It's just after four," I told the girl.

"Thanks," she said, kind of laughing to herself. And then she walked away. I don't know what was so funny.

Anyway, I started walking again and I hear the buzz of an airplane overhead. I look up and see that Sophie has taken off without me. I stand on the ground, watching her fly farther and farther away.

(Later.)

Just got off the phone with Molly. We're going out on an official date on Friday. Which means, according to Molly, that as of Friday we're officially "going out." We had this whole conversation about it.

—■—

"I've been thinking about it," Molly said. As usual, she'd called me. It's not that I don't want to call her; she just always calls me first. "It's time to move on to Phase Two."

"We're in Phase One now?" I asked.

"Yeah," Molly said. "Phase One is when we talk about going out."

"What's Phase Two?"

"Phase Two is when we go out," she said simply. "Actually, I thought we'd go out to dinner at Toasters. Talk for a while, maybe eat some hot food. Afterward maybe we could go dancing or something."

"So Phase Two is dinner and dancing?" I said. It didn't really sound all that great.

"You got it."

"How many phases are there?" I asked. "Is there a Phase Three?"

"There are at least nine phases. Let's not worry about the others yet," she said.

"So this means we're actually going out?" I said. "Once we begin Phase Two."

"Definitely. We're an item. A couple." She sounded really happy about it.

"And how is going out going to be different from what we've been doing so far?" I asked.

"You'll see," she said, in a teasing voice.

It's weird, for a person who claims that telling

—■—

the truth is so important, sometimes after I talk to Molly I don't feel like she's been honest with me at all. Sometimes what Molly says is even more obscure than what Thorne says, and he makes shit up constantly. At least with someone like Thorne you know where you stand.

Jan. 27, 5:15 P.M.

Honey is leaving on her Harvard road trip tomorrow, and I am definitely looking forward to having her out of the house for a while. For the last week she's been tinkering in her room with this big pile of metal. I asked her what she was doing, and she said, in this kind of irritated, aren't-you-an-idiot kind of voice, "What do you *think*, Wet One? I'm building a robot."

I stood in her doorway watching her untangle a big pile of wires at her desk. There was a soldering iron on the floor, and a suitcase was lying open on her unmade bed, with nothing in it.

"You're building a robot?" I repeated.

"Hey, Electra, there's an echo in here," Honey said to the pile of wires.

—■—

"Electra? That's its name?"

Honey looked up at me through these Plexiglas eye-protector things she was wearing. "*Her* name," she said.

I just looked at the pile of wires. It didn't look like Electra had much of a body or anything. She was just a bunch of wires and transistors and circuit boards.

"Why are you building a robot?" I asked.

Honey picked up the soldering iron and jiggled it. "Two reasons. First, 'cause we have to do these stupid-ass senior projects. This one's mine. Second, because I can."

I looked at the mass of wires again. "What does she do?"

"Do?" Honey said. "Do?"

"Yeah," I said. "What's her purpose."

Honey shrugged. "She says stuff," she said.

"Like what?"

She put down the soldering iron and connected two loose wires. There was a kind of spark, and then this disembodied, breathy voice said, "A merry heart maketh a cheerful countenance."

Honey disconnected the wires and the voice stopped.

"Jesus, Honey," I said. "No wonder you got into Harvard."

She stood up and glared at me. "Would you shut up about Harvard already?"

"I see your packing is going really well," I said, looking at the empty suitcase.

"You want me to pack?" she said. "Fine, I'll pack." She picked up the whole pile of wires and circuit boards and threw it in the suitcase, along with the soldering iron and a screwdriver. Then she went to her underwear drawer and opened it. "You think they wear bras at Harvard?" she asked.

"Probably," I said. "The girls do, anyway."

"Yeah," she said. "You're probably right. Probably *everybody* wears goddamn bras." She pulled her underwear drawer out of her bureau and dumped its contents into the suitcase. Then she threw the drawer on the floor, and zipped up the suitcase. "Okay," she said. "Now I'm packed."

"Hey, Honey," I said. "Can I just say one thing?"

"What?" she said. She was really pissed off at me. It was kind of entertaining.

"If you don't want to go to Harvard, why don't you just tell them you don't want to go? Why don't you do what you want to do?"

"Yeah, okay, fine," she said. "I'll just e-mail the admissions office right now and tell them I'm not coming because what I really want to do is hang out with lowlife losers in Pompano and sleep in a trailer."

—■—

"I'm serious," I said. "You don't have to go to Harvard."

"But that is what I want to do," she said. "Don't you get it?"

"You really do want to go to Harvard?"

"No, Pistachio Nuts. I really do want to lie around Pompano in a trailer with lowlife losers. That's what I like to do. Hang out with my friends and watch television. Eat Doritos. Play cards. But you're not allowed to do that if you're me. Oh, no, you have to go to goddamn Massachusetts and learn Latin and Swedish for four years."

"Honey," I said. "You already *know* Latin. You're *fluent* in Latin."

"I know," she yelled. "I'm fluent in goddamn Swedish, too. You think I like being smart? Jesus!"

"I'm just saying you don't have to go to Harvard," I said. "It's your life."

"And I'm saying you're wrong. It's not my life. I *do* have to go." She glared at me again, all annoyed.

I knew Honey didn't mean what she was saying. If she had to stay in Pompano next year, she'd go crazy. I think Honey really does want to go to Harvard. I think she can't wait to go there. For once in her life she's going to fit in. Here in Pompano, Honey is a world all her own. None of her friends have half her brains, and none of the geniuses in

—— ■ ——

her special classes are into the stuff she's into. But maybe Honey's afraid that at Harvard everybody's going to be just like her, and for once in her life she isn't going to be special. Maybe she's scared.

There was a voice from inside Honey's suitcase. *"Brzzzrp,"* it said. "Help me! Please help me!"

It reminded me of Sophie. Everything reminds me of her.

—■—

Jan. 28

Well, today was a pretty big day. I had that date with Molly and we had a fight. A big one. I'm not all that surprised, but it still makes me feel bad. I don't think we're going to be seeing each other anymore.

We met at Toasters, which is this new theme restaurant where every table has a little toaster oven on it, and you order your meal and they give you all sorts of stuff you can make in the toaster while you wait, including toast (of course) and Pop Tarts and waffles. Meanwhile, they're playing all this Dixieland music or something. The cheeseburgers were supposed to be really good so we ordered them, and a second later the waitress came by with hamburger buns.

—■—

"Okay, kids, you know what to do! Stick your buns in the oven and toast 'em!" she said. She was wearing a red checkered shirt with a name tag that said JUDY, and her hands were incredibly small, like little paws.

Molly was wearing a sparkly dress that was way too formal for Toasters, and she'd put her hair up on top of her head. I think she'd spent a lot of time preparing for this date, which made me think that maybe Molly doesn't really go out with guys very often. Maybe her whole act about being so sophisticated and everything was just a big fat lie.

It wasn't the best thing to be thinking when we were supposedly moving from Phase One to Phase Two.

"You know what I'd name a restaurant, if I had one?" Molly said when we sat down.

"What?" I was hoping she was going to say something nice, something that would get me out of the mood I was in and put us both at ease.

"Who Farted?" she said. Then she started laughing like this was hilarious. "Don't you think that's funny?" she said. "A restaurant called Who Farted? Wouldn't you eat there? I would!"

Something about the way she was laughing really annoyed me. I don't know. I just kept thinking that if Sophie were there instead of Molly we'd be looking into each other's eyes and not talking at all.

"Oh, no," Molly said. "There you go off to Mars again. You know I hate it when you suddenly leave for outer space and leave me sitting by myself on earth. It's lonely."

"Sorry," I said.

"You didn't like my joke."

I shrugged. "It's nothing," I said. "I'm just kind of spaced out that's all."

"Sexual frustration. All that testosterone has blocked up your system and messed with your head," Molly said. She kind of smirked when she said that.

I caught a glimpse of myself in the mirror on the other side of the restaurant, and I thought, I don't look so bad. Why is she being so mean to me? I was wearing a new button-down short-sleeved shirt I got at Pac Sun and a pair of jeans. I'd just shaved. I mean, I didn't look like a rock star or anything, but I thought I looked like someone a girl would want to be seen with. But Molly was making me feel bad. Even the way she'd dressed up so much made me feel like I hadn't made enough of an effort.

"They say testosterone makes boys think about sex every fifteen seconds. Is that true Jonah?" Molly continued.

I smiled, but it was a totally fake smile. I didn't

feel like smiling. All I could think about was how Sophie, as weird as she was, was never mean to me. I remembered when Sophie and I were in the hotel in Orlando and how her hair smelled when she leaned her head against my chest.

"Maybe every ten seconds?" Molly said.

I didn't say anything.

The toaster went off and Molly took out our hamburger buns. She put one on her plate and nibbled the other one. "Mmm," she said. "What delicious buns you have, Jonah!" She held up her bun. "Would you like to have a bite of mine?"

I picked up the bottle of EZ Squirt green ketchup and suddenly pointed it at Molly like it was a gun. I imagined giving it a big squeeze, and the green ketchup spewing all over Molly's sparkly dress. I didn't do it, but Molly, of course, knew exactly what I was thinking. We just looked at each other for a second, surprised.

Then I stood up and said, "I'm going." I hadn't even known I was going to do it until I did it, but once I was on my feet I knew it was the right thing.

"You're going where?" Molly said. "You don't have a car. You don't even have a bike." She smiled. "Since I crushed it."

"I'm walking."

—■—

I turned away and started walking through Toasters. Molly got up and followed me. "Wait," she said. "Jonah Black. Stop. What are you doing?"

"What does it look like?" I said.

She followed me outside. "Jonah," she said. "I'm sorry. I wasn't trying to upset you. I was just being myself. You know me. I can be kind of a jerk sometimes."

"You got that right," I said. All I wanted was to be away from her.

"But I don't mean it. You know I don't. Jonah, please stop and look at me," Molly begged.

But I didn't stop and look at her. I was tired of her telling me what to do all the time.

"Jonah, you've lost your sense of humor!" she said, and laughed, but her laugh sounded kind of sad and desperate. People in the parking lot were staring at her. She looked totally out of place in her spangly dress in the parking lot of a Toasters restaurant. For a second, I felt sorry for her. What I was doing seemed really mean all of a sudden. But I kept on walking.

"I don't want you to walk away," Molly said, her voice choking. "Jonah, please don't go." I knew she was about to cry, and I'd never seen her cry before. But still, I didn't stop.

"I'm sorry," she said, and that was the last thing

——■——

I heard her say. I kept walking until I got all the way to the beach and started heading toward home. It was a long walk.

As I walked up the beach, I looked at the waves churning in the moonlight and listened to the ocean roar. I wasn't entirely sure I hadn't just done something wrong.

Let's say Molly really was full of it and she really had put on this whole act. The reason she'd done it was because she was unsure of herself. And there's nothing abnormal about that. Maybe I was being totally unfair. The truth is, I don't even know Molly that well. I've never been to her house or met her parents or any of her friends. I guess that would have been part of Phase Two, but now that's not going to happen. I don't know. How is it possible that you really like someone one day and then the next day, everything about them suddenly bugs you?

It was kind of weird to be walking by the ocean with my jeans and shoes on. I took my shoes off and let the surf rush up and around my ankles, until the bottom three inches of my pants were soaked. The water was really cold, but I didn't care. It felt good.

I walked past the Dune, and smiled as I thought about Posie knocking Kassandra's plane out of

—— ■ ——

the sky. Posie and Lamar had a little fight about Kassandra after the diving meet, but they've cleared things up. It's nice that she and Lamar have each other, I guess.

Then I thought about Amelia Earhart, and Sophie looking out the window of Maggins wishing she could fly. I realized she'd written me all these letters and I hadn't written her back once. Every day she probably checked the mailbox and it was always empty.

As I walked by Niagara Towers, I suddenly decided to stop in and see Pops Berman. It had been a while since we'd talked. The receptionist buzzed me in and I asked her which apartment Pops Berman lived in. She said to go up to the twelfth floor.

I got up to Pops's floor and walked down the hall. I hated the way the place smelled, like floor wax and disease and loneliness. Pops calls it Viagra Towers, but it didn't seem like anyone in that place was taking too much Viagra. It seemed like a place where people go to die.

I rang Pops's bell and he opened it quickly. "Hey, Chipper," he said. He didn't look as bad as I'd thought he would. He was wearing a white bathrobe and his Red Sox cap and these strange Japanese slippers. He looked me up and down. "Oh, no," he said. "You've done it again."

———■———

I walked into his apartment. "I'm all right," I said. I looked around his living room, and it was nothing like what I expected. It was really nice! He had an Oriental rug and lots of pictures on a mantelpiece above a gas fireplace. There were old baseball photographs on one wall. I'd been expecting dirty dishes in the sink and one bare light bulb hanging down on a wire.

He went to the kitchen and got us both glasses of milk, then he sat down next to me on the brown leather couch. "Got milk?" he said, without smiling.

"Pops—" I said.

"Three glasses a day," he said. "You need calcium. I'm not kidding you. Three glasses." I picked up my glass and sipped.

"Mmm," I said. I hate milk.

"Shut up," he said. "You don't like it, pour it down the toilet. You want your bones to snap like little twigs, go ahead. I don't care." He leaned forward. "Now tell me what's what."

"You seem better," I said. "I was really worried about you for a while."

"Better, worse," Pops said, and shrugged. "What's the difference? I'm not hockin' up balls o' mucus anyway. That's something."

"Well, good," I said, taking another sip of milk. "Now tell me. What's what?"

—— ■ ——

"Well, I've been sort of seeing this really smart girl named Molly," I explained. "She can be nice and I thought I really liked her, but she has kind of a mean streak. And she has this big thing about always telling the truth all the time. If she thinks you're telling her a load of crap, she goes nuts."

"Oh, yes," said Pops Berman. "I used to call them girls Blue Fairies." He drank about half the glass of milk and licked his upper lip so he wouldn't have a milk mustache. "You know, Pinocchio always used to get hit on the head with a rolling pin whenever he told a lie. And Blue Fairy would always bail him out, but he had to promise her not to ever lie to her." He finished the rest of his milk and wiped his mouth with the back of his hand. "You gotta watch out for girls like that. A lot of the time these girls who only tell the truth are more full of crap than the liars are."

I nodded. "I think I'm starting to figure that out."

I looked over at the wall of baseball photos again, and suddenly I realized. The guy in the pictures was Pops. In a Red Sox uniform.

I sat up. "I didn't know you played with the Red Sox, Pops," I said. "That's really you, isn't it?"

"Yeah. What, you're all surprised I wasn't always some broken down old windbag?" he said.

I stood up to look at the pictures more carefully.

—■—

Pops got up and stood next to me. I could hear him breathing heavily.

"So, how long did you play ball for?" I asked him.

"I was in the majors three years. Minors for five. I broke my wrist. Then I joined the fire department."

"What position did you play?" I said, still amazed.

"Shortstop."

Pops didn't look all that different in the photos. His hair was brown, but his face was all wrinkled and leathery even then. One of the photographs showed him sliding into base with a big cloud of dust around him. It was pretty cool.

"She walk your doggy yet, Chipper?" Pops asked.

I shrugged.

Pops wheezed into his hand and pounded his chest with his fist. "Oh, no," he said. "Not again."

"Molly says sex isn't important," I said, like that explained everything.

Pops kept wheezing, his face was turning red. "Not—not important?"

He sat back down on the couch.

"That's what she says." I sank into the couch next to him.

"You believe that?" Pops asked me.

I turned to look at him. It was funny, he looked

—■—

a lot younger now. Maybe seeing those pictures of him made me see him in another light. "No," I said. "I mean, I don't think it's the most important thing in the world, but I do think it's—"

"The hell it's not important!" Pops said. He slapped me on the leg with a bristly hand. "You hear me?!"

"I hear you," I said. Probably half the people on his floor could hear him.

"What about the basket case?" Pops said. "The mopsy top?"

"Sophie," I said.

There was a long silence. I heard someone else coughing in the apartment next door. I wondered if everyone in Niagara Towers was sick. It gave me the creeps. Even though Pops's apartment was nice, it still a lonely, depressing place. I thought about Pops standing out on the balcony, watching the ocean night after night, and wondered what he thought about. His dead wife, probably. The only woman he ever loved.

"She still shut up in that rich kid's nut-hatch?" Pops asked.

"Yeah," I said.

"She still wanna walk your doggy?"

"She says she does," I told him.

"You gonna go and see her?" he said.

I looked out the window. There was the cold,

January Atlantic, almost black now as the clouds covered over the moon.

"Jonah," Pops said. I think it's the first time he's ever called me by my real name. "Listen," he said, and his voice was very quiet now. I could hear the ticking of a clock on his mantelpiece, the waves outside crashing on the beach. "Listen to that little doggy. You can't hear him because you're such a rockhead, but he's there."

I kept looking out the window and watching the water. I thought about Sophie's house in Maine. A lighthouse flashing through fog.

"Are you listening?" Pops said.

"Yes," I said.

"You hear him? Your little doggy?"

"Yeah," I said.

"Well all right then," whispered Pops.

I stood up. "I have to go," I told Pops. "I'm sorry. I have to—"

"Don't apologize." Pops clapped me on the shoulder. "Okay, Chipper," he said. "Good luck."

Soon I was walking up the beach again. I got home about an hour later. Honey was leaning against the side of her Jeep, looking at her watch. "Thank God," she said. "I was about to give up on you."

"Why?"

"Come on," she said. "Get your stuff. I told Mom you were coming, too. She's excited for you."

———■———

"You told Mom? But I didn't even—I mean, how did you—?"

"Aw come on, Squirrel Nuts. You're easier to read than Dr. Seuss. Come on," she patted the front seat of her Jeep. "Kiss Ma and jump on in. Assuming you can pry her off of Robere."

I walked into the house in a total daze, thinking about how everybody seems to knows me better than I know myself. Mom and Mr. Bond were sitting cross-legged on the floor. Mr. Bond was holding Mom's breasts again. "Chong!" he said. "CHONG!!!!"

"Mom—" I said.

"Sshh, Jonah," Mom whispered. "I'm on deadline."

"I just wanted you to know—"

"It's fine, Jonah. Honey told me. You go have fun," said Mom.

"Okay," I said. It's weird, but I kind of wanted her to want me to stay. "You're sure this is okay? I'm going to miss some school."

"Jonah," Mom said, crossly. "You're distorting the energy!"

"CHONNGG!" said Mr. Bond with his eyes closed. It looked like he was squeezing Mom's boobs kind of hard.

"Okay," I said. "I'll call you from Dad's house."

"I love you, Jonah," Mom said. "Remember to be nice to yourself!"

—— ■ ——

“Okay,” I said. “I will.”

I went into my room and threw some things into my backpack. The last thing I grabbed were the cans of peaches and the crushed tomatoes, so I could do my broken-arm recovery exercises on the road.

I went outside and got in the front seat next to Honey. She was already behind the wheel with the engine idling. A cigarette dangled from her lips. The moment I pulled my door closed she backed out of the driveway at like, ninety miles an hour.

I noticed the crushed azaleas in the front yard, and I had a quick, sad thought about Molly. I hoped I was doing the right thing.

“Road trip,” screamed Honey, revving into fifth gear. As we approached the drawbridge, the warning lights started to flash. The bridge was going up. “Yeah, right,” Honey snarled, and drove straight on through the flashing lights. Other cars honked at her, but she just kept on going, and we made it to the other side before the drawbridge even started to rise.

Honey hunted around on the floor for a CD. “Cradle of Filth,” she said, and stuck the disc in the slot. Sick music poured from the speakers. I put my sun visor down. We were off.

—■—

Jan. 29, 1 P.M.

On the road with Honey, North Carolina. We're back in the car and driving north after spending last night in a motel near Daytona Beach. It was a pretty gruesome place, too—a little dive next to a bar. Honey thought it was the greatest place on earth, and we actually had to pass three or four much nicer hotels before she found one that disgusting. There were cockroaches crawling around in the shower, short curly hairs on the sheets, and lots of surly-looking guys on motorcycles out in the parking lot all night. I had to listen to them revving their Harleys until dawn and really only got some sleep this morning in the car after we left.

I woke up right as we were crossing the border into North Carolina. It's greener here than in Florida, and a lot less flat. There are mountains but no palm trees. And there are horses everywhere.

Honey looked over at me and said, "Good morning, Merry Sunshine."

She turned up the volume on the CD player and we drove on listening to the music for a while. If you can call it music. I liked looking out the window and watching the world go by. It reminded me of this trip we took to Yellowstone Park before Mom and Dad got divorced. I liked driving cross-country a lot more than being in the park itself.

"So tell me this, Stringbean," said Honey after a while. She turned down the music. "What are we going to do about Tiffany?"

"What do you mean?" I said. "She's Dad's wife. We don't have to do anything about her."

Honey frowned. "I thought you said she was a cretin."

"I didn't say that."

"You told me she's like, twenty-five years old. She rides horses. Has lots of rich-girl hobbies. What else does she do? Redecorates the house every month, that sort of thing?"

I shrugged. "She's not so bad."

Honey smiled her evil smile. "You know what, Jonah, I think she is that bad. The only question is, What are we going to do about her?"

———■———

"You're really determined to make a good impression on Dad, aren't you?"

"Well," Honey said. "He's definitely knocked himself out reaching out to me, hasn't he?" She punched in the cigarette lighter and stuck a Camel into her mouth.

"What do you want from him?" I said. "He's moved on. Just like Mom."

"Jeez, aren't you Mr. Understanding," Honey said. The madder she got, the faster she drove. I wasn't so sure I wanted her to get madder.

"What's that supposed to mean?" I said.

"You know what I think? I think you're more pissed off at Dad than I am. You just won't admit it," Honey accused.

"What am I supposed to admit?" I said.

"That you resent him. Because he ditched us," she said, and lit her cigarette.

I looked out the window. We passed a billboard for something called Indian Spirit Caverns. I thought about that trip to Yellowstone. On the way back from the West we'd visited Mammoth Caves. It was very cool. There's a picture somewhere of me and Honey and Mom and Dad standing by the stalactites in this blue light.

"Maybe he did ditch us," I said. "What are we supposed to do about it? I mean, it happened. They

—— ■ ——

got divorced. Now we live in Florida and Dad lives in Pennsylvania, and he's married to Tiffany and Mom's dating Mr. Bond."

"I'll tell you what we're supposed to do about it," Honey shouted. She pushed the accelerator to the floor and the Jeep roared even louder. We must have been going over a hundred. "We make them pay," Honey said, between her teeth.

I didn't say anything more and finally Honey eased up a bit on the accelerator. She reached down between the seats and got out a book and handed it to me. "Hey, Jonah, look through this book. Tell me if we're near anything."

The book was titled *The 100 Strangest Places in America.* It was a big list of all these places you could visit, like the World's Biggest Coffee Pot and the Monkey Orphanage. In Fort Mitchell, Kentucky, was the Home for Retired Ventriloquists' Dummies. "There's Indian Spirit Caverns," I said. "That's only about twenty-five miles away."

"Caves? Nah. Caves don't do anything for me," Honey said, waving her cigarette in the air. "Do you like caves?"

"I don't know. They're all right, I guess. Hey, do you remember that time we all went to Mammoth Caves, on the way back from Yellowstone?" I asked.

"What?"

—— ▪ ——

"When we went to Yellowstone. We stopped at Mammoth Caves on the way back," I reminded her.

"I didn't go to Mammoth Caves," Honey said. "I didn't go to Yellowstone, either."

"Honey," I said. "We have pictures of us there. This was just before the divorce. Mom and Dad fought the whole way in the car as we were driving west."

"I wasn't there," Honey said and turned the music up again.

Sometimes I think Honey and I grew up in different families.

(Later. Somewhere in Tennessee.)

I've been doing my arm exercises while we drive north and I'm almost done with the canned peaches. My arm still hurts, though.

We just had lunch in this diner near the Smoky Mountains called Sam's. I love diners. And I liked everything about Sam's—the pink uniforms the waitresses wore, the round lime-green stools at the counter, the little mini-jukeboxes at the table with the OUT OF ORDER signs, the round glass canisters for sugar, and the little stand where they stack up the jelly packets. At the counter an overweight, balding man was smoking a cigarette and eating meat-

—— ■ ——

loaf at the same time. An ambulance drove by and he turned around to watch it pass. He was wearing a T-shirt that said HARVARD BUSINESS SCHOOL. I wonder if he just got the T-shirt at the Salvation Army or if he really went there. If he did go there he didn't look like he'd gotten much out of it.

Honey was watching the guy, too. She got this weird look on her face. She pushed her home fries around in the runny yellow goo of her eggs.

"What?" I said.

"You know what," she said.

"It's not going to be that bad," I said.

"You know what, Weinerdog?" she said. "It's going to be *exactly* that bad."

She ate a big forkful of eggs and some of the yolk ran down her chin. She dabbed herself with a napkin, then crumpled it into a ball and let it drop onto the counter. I took a bite of my silver-dollar pancakes.

"I know what you're afraid of," I said, looking at her. "About Harvard, I mean."

"Shut up," suggested Honey.

"I know," I insisted.

"I don't care," she said. "I don't want to talk about it."

"You shouldn't be worried about fitting in there," I said, ignoring her. "You'll be fine."

——■——

Honey looked at me like I was a medical curiosity. "What's this now?" she said. "Believe it or not, I'm lost."

"No, you're not," I said.

She kind of squinted at me. "So you think the reason I don't want to go to Harvard is that everybody up there is going to be like me? That I'm going to walk into a classroom, and all the girls are going to look just like me, like my music, want to do the stuff I like to do?"

I nodded. "I think that's possible. It'll be good for you, though. It'll be nice for you not to have to stick out for once. You know, be the freak."

"You think I'm not going to be the freak up there?" she said, shaking her head. "Man, are you confused."

"You're not going to be the only freak. There will be lots of them," I said. "But that's good. I think you'll like it."

"Woohoo!" Honey yelled, The guy at the counter looked over at us. So did everyone else in the restaurant.

"Harvard's not going to be any better," she said. "It's going to be worse. You know what people are like at Harvard?"

"Not really," I said.

"Love Story," she said. "You ever see that movie?"

"No." It sounded corny.

Honey rolled her eyes. "You didn't miss much. This chick goes out with this hockey player. They all walk around wearing tweed. The only good thing about the movie is, she dies of cancer in the end." She took another bite of her eggs. "That's what Harvard's going to be like."

I smiled. "You won't get cancer," I said. "If that's what you're worried about."

"Shut up," Honey told me.

The waitress came over. She was wearing a name tag that said AGLET, which is a name I'd never heard before. "How's everybody doing?" she asked.

Honey and I both answered in unison. "Fine."

(Later. Fort Mitchell, Kentucky.)

Okay, let me just say the Museum for Retired Ventriloquists' Dummies is actually really cool. They have like, three hundred dummies in there, in a bunch of different rooms. In one room they're all sitting in chairs, like kids in an auditorium. In another they're sitting on bleachers. And all of them are looking back at you, staring. They have tags on their toes, too, like corpses, and the tags say what their name is and what the name of the ventriloquist was who owned each one.

—■—

Honey thought this was just about the greatest place she'd ever seen in her life. She kept walking around with this big smile on her face, as if she'd finally seen something that surprised her. That doesn't happen very often.

Our tour guide was the widow of the guy who originally collected the dummies.

"Can you make them talk?" Honey asked her.

"No," she said, kind of sadly. "I don't know how to do it."

"Do what?"

"Throw my voice," she said. "My husband was the ventriloquist, but he's not with us anymore."

"Man! They're so incredibly creepy," Honey said, awestruck.

"I don't find them creepy," said the woman.

"Yeah, well," Honey said. "Let me tell you, you're wrong. They are wicked creepy."

Later we were sitting in front of the museum eating hot dogs. Honey had that new green ketchup all over hers. "You think her husband ditched her?" she asked.

"I think he died," I said. "She said he 'wasn't with us anymore.' I think that means he's dead."

Honey shook her head. "I think that means he ran off with somebody. Maybe some other ventriloquist. You think somebody with that many dummies wants to hang around with some chick who can't even throw her voice? I don't think so."

"Well, if he did take off, he left the dummies behind," I pointed out.

"He probably took all the good ones with him," Honey said, and stuffed the rest of her hot dog in her mouth. She chewed it, deep in thought.

"'Course, you know what," she said. "If you're a good enough ventriloquist you don't need anybody else. You know what I mean? You can just do the voices of everyone you want to hang out with and be left alone." She sounded really sad, in her own twisted way.

"That's deep," I said.

"Shut up," said Honey.

"Maybe I should get you a dummy for Christmas this year," I said.

"Too late, kid," said Honey. "I'm going to be at Harvard, remember? They got all the dummies I need."

Anyway, I'm glad we stopped at the dummy museum. It made me think about Amelia Earhart and her trip around the globe. I guess she must have seen some pretty unusual stuff, too.

—■—

Jan. 30. Ohio.

Another crummy motel last night, although this one was nowhere near as disgusting as the one in Daytona. This one was just the standard boring ice-machine-in-the-hallway kind of place. I think there are about eight million other hotels exactly like it, all across the country. At least it was clean.

Because I can't drive, there's not a lot for me to do on this trip besides look out the window and think, and I'm not sure that's a good thing for me. I keep thinking about Molly and wondering if I should have handled things differently. Maybe if I'd told her what I was thinking and told her she was getting on my nerves, we could have talked about it and worked things out. But I was just too mad at her. I guess I've screwed up another perfectly good relationship.

Of course I keep thinking about Sophie, too. I've definitely figured out that I need to know the deal with her before I can really have a relationship with anybody else. I just can't get Sophie out of my head. That's what wrecked things with Posie, and basically that's what's wrecking things with Molly, too.

But maybe I'm not supposed to have a relationship with someone else. Maybe Sophie and I are meant for each other.

But what if Sophie is just plain nuts? I mean, every time I've had anything to do with her, things got pretty weird pretty fast. And I don't think I was meant to be with a total schizo. But maybe I can help her. She deserves that.

Oh, God. I think I'm in love with her.

Honey just took out the Cradle of Filth CD, which we've listened to about eight million times now, and put in Flathead, which we've only listened to about nine million times. And she's chain smoking, which she doesn't usually do. I think she's nervous about seeing Dad, and probably nervous about going up to Harvard, too. I'm kind of nervous, too, but for entirely different reasons.

(Later. Outside Brook Park, Ohio, heading east on the Ohio Turnpike.)

Okay. The World's Largest Monopoly Board turned out to be a parking lot. And we almost got into a fight there. We were walking around the parking lot, which instead of numbers in the lot is organized with signs that say BOARDWALK or B&O RAILROAD or PARK PLACE, and the guy who ran it was kind of annoyed that we were walking around looking at it. He kept hassling us because he thought we were car thieves. He didn't even believe us when we said that his parking lot was listed in the book of 100 strangest places in America.

Honey almost threw a punch at the guy, and I thought he was going to call the police. Fortunately, at that point I found the book and showed the guy where his parking lot was listed, but he still wasn't all that impressed. We didn't spend very much time there.

That was about two hours ago, and now we're going east on the Ohio Turnpike. Stopping at all these weirdo places has added a lot of time to our drive, but I don't mind. I'm not even sure of what I'm going to do when I get there.

About an hour ago, Honey and I had this conversation:

———■———

"So, Honey," I said. "Remember when you said that what you really wanted to do, instead of go to Harvard, was hang out with Pompano losers, watching TV all day? Did you mean that?"

"I don't know," Honey said. "Sometimes, definitely. I like watching TV."

"Well, who knows?" I said. "Maybe there are some losers at Harvard you can hang out with."

"Not likely." She punched in the lighter to light up her four hundredth cigarette.

"Well, wait until you get there. I bet you're going to meet some of the biggest losers you've ever seen in your life." I told her.

A slow smile crept across Honey's face. "You really think so?" she said.

"Definitely."

"Well, then," Honey said. "I guess I have something to look forward to."

Then, from the back seat, came this voice. "It is a wise man who *zrpfft* can stay cool, even in hell." I kind of freaked out for a second, but then I remembered Electra. She was talking from Honey's suitcase.

Jan. 31. Bryn Mawr, Pennsylvania.

This is really strange. I'm writing this in my bedroom in Dad's house, and it's got some of my stuff in it, even though I never really lived here. Honey and I got in last night about 3 A.M. and we snuck in through the dog door and crept up the stairs and went to bed. Dad still doesn't know we're coming. So here we are at 9:30 A.M. on a Saturday and I can hear someone in the shower—probably Tiffany—and in a little while Honey and I are going to go downstairs to the kitchen and shock the hell out of them. Wait, I think I hear Honey's footsteps in the hall.

(Later.)

Whoa! Okay. A lot has happened in the last hour and a half.

After I heard Honey's footsteps I suddenly heard this high-pitched yipping sound, followed by a scream. It was Tiffany's toy poodle, Cuddles, barking when he discovered Honey on the stairs. Then Tiffany screamed when she followed Cuddles out into the hallway and found Honey sliding down the banister smoking a cigarette. She probably scared Tiffany half to death. Honey is a particularly scary sight in the morning, especially to someone with a name like Tiffany, whose primary activity each week is getting her nails done.

Cuddles kept barking and barking, and Honey yelled, "Call off the rat, lady," and Tiffany said, "Who are you? What are you doing here? I'm calling the police!" and Honey said, "I said call off the rat!" and then I heard a *thunk*, which was the sound Cuddles made when Honey kicked him across the hallway. Tiffany screamed again and went upstairs into her bedroom. Cuddles went after Honey again and bit her in the ankle, and Honey started screaming and shaking her leg around trying to get rid of the dog, who was holding on with a viselike grip. Then Tiffany came back out of the bedroom with a little revolver pointed at Honey. "If you don't leave, I'm going to have to shoot," she told her. But Honey ignored her. She just kept kicking the dog around. That's when I

———■———

came downstairs and Dad came out of the shower with a towel wrapped around him and stood at the top of the stairs. Everyone was shouting and barking and finally Dad yelled, "EVERYBODY SHUT UP!!!"

There was quiet for a second, except for Cuddles, and Dad said, "Tiffany, you know Jonah. And this is my daughter, Honor Elspeth." Tiffany looked at us suspiciously and Honey said, "You can put the gun away, Mom." Tiffany grabbed Cuddles by the collar and went into her bedroom with the dog and the gun and closed the door and locked it.

"Jesus Christ, look at my leg," said Honey. It was all gouged with teeth marks. Honey looked like she wanted to cry but she didn't want to do it in public.

Dad stood there for a second looking down at the two of us, with the towel wrapped around him.

"Hi, Dad," I said. "We're college visiting."

Dad nodded and said, "Good for you."

"I think I need to go to the hospital," said Honey.

"Lawrence," said Tiffany through the door. "Lawrence, I need you."

Dad looked at us sadly for a moment, then he went into the bedroom and closed the door.

———■———

"Well," I told Honey, "I think that went pretty well."

"I have to go to the hospital," Honey said. She limped downstairs. "When I come back, I'm going to murder that bitch." I wasn't sure whether she meant Cuddles or Tiffany.

Honey got in the Jeep and drove off to the Bryn Mawr hospital. I got myself a bowl of cereal and sat down in Dad's kitchen and read the comics in the *Philadelphia Inquirer*, which has more comics in it than just about any paper I've ever seen. I checked out my horoscope, too, which said it would be a good day for renewing old acquaintances. I hoped they were referring to someone other than Dad.

Then I walked around the house for a little bit. It's just amazing how huge it is. The first floor has a living room that's about the size of our whole house in Pompano. There's a piano that no one plays and shelves and shelves of bookcases covered with books that no one reads. There's a chandelier in the central hallway, and through the door to the right is a long dining room where no one eats, and through another archway is a family room that no one sits in. You go through another alcove and there's what Dad calls the conservatory, which is this eight-sided glass room with a table in it

---

where you read the paper and drink coffee. Just off the conservatory is a huge kitchen with a brick oven that no one cooks in, and all these cabinets made by the Pennsylvania Dutch. I've always thought Dad's house would be great for a party, as long as Dad wasn't home.

Dad came down the stairs after a while and sat down at the table in the conservatory with a cup of coffee and the business section of the *Inquirer.* I got a glass of juice and brought it in and sat with him.

"Well, you two made quite an entrance," he said with a wry chuckle. His smile brought out all these lines in his face that I didn't remember being there before. Dad looks older. He has more gray hair and he wears these new thick glasses that kind of magnify the wrinkles around his eyes. He had a little shaving cream on one ear. I thought about telling him it was there but then I decided it would be more fun if I didn't.

"I'm sorry, Dad," I said. "We got in late last night and we thought we'd surprise you."

"You did that all right," said Dad. "I don't think Tiffany's going to come down for a while."

"I guess we should have called."

"I guess you should have," Dad said. His whole nice-guy-Dad demeanor kind of evaporated, and I

—— ■ ——

realized how much effort it had been for him to maintain it.

"Do you think it's possible one time," he said, and he sounded really angry, "that you could be part of our lives without creating a federal disaster area? Just once?" His throat was turning red now. The last time I'd seen him look like this was when I got thrown out of Masthead Academy. That was the last time I'd seen him. I guess it did seem like every time he's heard from me recently there's been some major scene.

"I told you we wanted to surprise you," I said lamely. "Honey's visiting Harvard and I decided to come along to see you, and maybe visit some of my friends up here. We didn't mean to make a scene."

"Tiffany isn't well," Dad said "She needs rest. And just like that, you and Honor bring this . . . this calamity to our home."

"Well, we didn't mean to—"

"Jonah!" Dad yelled. "You can't just walk in here unannounced."

"What's wrong with Tiffany?" I said. "Is she sick?"

Dad drank his coffee, and the red burning color faded out of his neck. "She's pregnant, Jonah. Pregnant."

———■———

"Ah," I said. I let this sink in. It seemed kind of sad to me, Tiffany being pregnant, and then I realized that Dad was the father. I don't know why I didn't get this at first, but I didn't.

Dad smiled. "That's right Jonah. You're going to have a brother."

"A brother?"

Dad nodded. "We did the ultrasound. It's a boy. Lawrence Hopkins Black, Junior."

Without thinking, I got up and went over to Dad and gave him a big hug. He didn't know what to do for a second, then he put his coffee cup down and hugged me back.

"Congratulations, Dad," I said. "That's awesome."

"Well," Dad said. I could tell he was surprised by my hug. "Thank you, Jonah."

Then Dad poured milk into his bowl of Raisin Bran and opened his newspaper. I know Dad well enough to know that that meant our conversation was over.

I went back upstairs and plugged my laptop into the jack in my bedroom, or the room that Tiffany has tried to make feel like my bedroom. It's sad, she has no idea what sort of things I actually like. The walls are papered with blue sailboats on a light blue background and the rug is dark red. On the bed is this red, white, and blue patchwork quilt.

———■———

She's put Philadelphia Eagles pennants on the wall, and a framed picture of me diving at Masthead last year. It's not a bad room, actually, it's just weird that it's supposed to be mine when I've never really lived in it.

I logged on to AOL and there was a bunch of mail.

The first one was from Betsy Donnelly:

To: JBlack94710@aol.com
From: BetsD8@MastheadAcademy.edu

Jonah, I am sorry I didn't get a chance to write you before now. I went on the Masthead trip to Russia over Christmas so I've been away for almost five weeks. I got a TON of e-mail while I was gone and now I'm actually getting back to everyone. Sorry it took me so long.

Listen, nobody here knows what's up with Sophie anymore. The people in Maggins won't let anybody in to see her. What I heard is that she's really not all that sick, they're just keeping her in there just so she can kind of get some rest and perspective. If that's true it's pretty horrible, because Maggins isn't the kind of place you'd rest very well or get any decent perspective.

I want to know more about what happened over Christmas break. Sophie said she was going to see you in Orlando and that you were going to stay in this hotel or

———▪———

something, but then right after she got back she went into Maggins and nobody knows what happened. Did she freak out or something when you were together? You really have the touch! :)

Anyway, I can't WAIT to graduate. Mr. Woodward made sure we all had our applications out by the fifteenth of January and now everyone is waiting for their college acceptance letters.

The only other thing I should tell you is that Sullivan is back at Masthead. I guess he only had to do a semester away and now he's back, and supposedly he's reformed. It's really creepy. He's gone around to all the girls he took advantage of and apologized to them. When he did it to me he definitely didn't seem like he was for real. He's just saying he's sorry because he has to, not because he really IS. But now we have to look at Sullivan all the time, walking around like he's turned over a new leaf and he's all sensitive now. It bothers me even more than when he was just a jerk because I think he might be up to something.

I know he went to Maggins so he could see Sophie, but don't worry, they wouldn't let him in. They have pretty hard-core security there, and he's not on the clearance list. That's actually pretty impressive because I think Sullivan's dad is on the board at Maggins. Anyway, Sullivan says he hasn't given up trying because it's really important that he apologize to her. Personally I think he has other plans. She's the only girl who got away from him, thanks to you.

—— ■ ——

Anyway, enough trivia. I hope everything is going well down in Florida. I wish you would come up and visit some time. Really!!!

Love,
Bets

The next e-mail I got was from Molly:

To: JBlack94710@aol.com
From: Molly@turbonet.net

Jonah! Where are you?? I am SO SORRY. I was acting like a bitch yesterday and I bugged you and now nobody knows where you are and I am SO SORRY and I don't know what to do. I have never really felt like this about a boy before and I think that's what has made me act like such a bitch. It's like I'm really afraid I'm going to mess this up and so I act like a bitch so I won't have to feel like we're serious. But we are serious, at least I am. And I'm sorry I've been acting so bizarre. Does this make sense? I think I'm saying that the reason I've been so awful is because I really like you, and that scares me.

Will you write me back please and let me know what's up? Elanor Brubaker says that Thorne said you went to PA to see that girl Sophie. Please tell me that's not true!

WRITE ME NOW!!! IF YOU DON'T, WHEN YOU GET BACK, I'M GOING TO PUNCH YOU!!!

Then, a letter from Northgirl:

To: JBlack94710
From: Northgirl999

Jonah, everyone says you've left town, but nobody knows why. There are a lot of very funny rumors, including one that you have to appear in court because you're being tried for arson. Something to do with what went down when you got kicked out of school. There's another story that you got some girl pregnant.

I think I know you better than to believe that.

Anyway, I hope when you come back you're feeling better about life. I guess it's good that you're doing what you're doing. Assuming you're doing what I think you're doing, which I bet you are.

In my life—which I know you care oh so much about—I have a new boyfriend and I think we are going to have sex this weekend. I can't wait.

My only regret is, I wish it was you instead.

And the last one was from Sophie:

To: JBlack94710@aol.com
From: womens@Maggins.net

Jonah—Here I am all alone in a world of crazy people. I'm not crazy but if I stay in here much longer I will

——■——

be. Why do people think I'm crazy? I will tell you. It's because I love you, Jonah. You are the only person who ever sacrificed himself for me. I still can't believe you got kicked out of school so I wouldn't get into trouble. Except now I'm in trouble anyway. Do you hate me now? You don't write back. I don't even know if you know I'm alive. But I am alive, Jonah, and I am so alone. The other girls in here are schizophrenics and anorexics and they are really scary. This one girl said to me today, "I was just like you when I first came here. I thought I was getting out. But you get over that." Then she showed me her wrist where she'd cut herself. Jonah I am so scared and I don't think I'm going to make it. You probably won't even get this. Good-bye Jonah. Just remember I always loved you, okay? I never got to tell you like I wanted, or to show you. But maybe I should stop thinking about you. I can't even see your face anymore.

I hit reply and tried to send her a message back: *I'm closer than you think, Sophie. Hold on.* But the message kept coming back to me, Address Unknown. Must be some Maggins security thing.

I just read her e-mail again, and now I'm really upset. More than upset. I'm feeling totally sad and crazy and out of control.

I think I'm about to do something I'm going to regret later. But I'm going to do it anyway. I have to.

—■—

(Still Jan. 31, 11 P.M.)

Okay, here I am back in bed in this great bedroom of mine, writing about what turned out to be a very strange day. There's a lot to get down so I'm probably not going to be able to cover it all before I crash. But I better get started.

Anyway, I went and did the stupid thing I thought I was going to do, which turned out—big surprise—to be stupid. I stole Dad's Mercedes and drove it to Maggins.

Dad was in his bedroom with Tiffany and Cuddles when I came down the stairs, and I'd already decided I had to see Sophie immediately. I didn't want to ask for a ride and have to answer tons of questions from my dad about who I was visiting in Maggins, I didn't want to call a taxi for the same reasons, Honey had already taken off in her Jeep, and I sure as hell wasn't going to take the SEPTA bus down Lancaster Pike, which would have taken about a hundred years and stunk to hell. So I went downstairs and got the keys off the hook, and about two minutes after I read Sophie's e-mail I was in Dad's Mercedes driving down Conestoga toward Maggins.

I don't know why I don't have a license. My driving really isn't that bad. It's only when I kind of forget

—— ■ ——

about what I'm doing and start thinking about Sophie that I drive in the other lane, or go through stop signs or whatever. Driving with a truly terrible driver like Molly really put things in perspective. I mean, the worst thing I've ever done is drive the dean's car through the wall at the Beeswax Inn when I rescued Sophie from Sullivan. I'm sure Molly has done worse than that.

My arm isn't completely healed though, and driving makes it hurt. I've been doing the bicep curls with the can of crushed tomatoes but it still aches sometimes. I wonder if it's always going to hurt, like an old war wound. Something to remind me of Sophie forever and ever.

As I drove I turned on the radio. It's funny how radio stations can remind you of old times. WMMR is the big rock-and-roll station in Philly and just hearing the voice of the DJ reminded me of being at Masthead. But they were playing all this old stuff so I switched to WXPN, which was playing some nu-metal—no doubt one of Honey's bands. The song matched the mood I was in exactly.

Maggins is all the way down on City Line Avenue. It took about a half hour to get there, but it went by in a blur. The next thing I knew I was walking toward the front door of Maggins.

Maggins is in a big old three-story Victorian

—— ■ ——

building. Originally it was a private home, the home of Dr. Maggins, who went crazy. So they put him up in the attic and hired all these nurses to look after him. Over the years some other people moved their nutty relatives in with him, and pretty soon this kind of private arrangement had become a well-known psychiatric hospital for rich people, especially troubled teenagers and young adults who come from wealthy families who don't know what else to do with them. It's very exclusive. Getting into Maggins is even harder than getting into Harvard (although I'm sure Honey could get in without a problem).

I opened the door and walked in and there was a receptionist sitting at a wooden table in what looked like someone's living room, which I guess is what it once was.

The receptionist looked at me over the tops of her glasses. "Can I help you, sir?" she said.

"I'd like to see one of your patients," I told her.

"Who did you want to see?" she asked. There was this odd little smile on her lips.

"Sophie," I said, and for a second I choked on her last name. I never think of her as anything other than "Sophie." There was a long silence, and finally I added "O'Brien."

"Ah," said the receptionist, as if the fact that I

—■—

was looking for Sophie explained everything about me. It was like something went *click* in her mind, and I knew she wasn't going to let me in.

"What is your name, sir?"

"Jonah," I said. "Jonah Black."

"Mr. Black, Sophie is on restricted visitation. Only individuals who have been cleared by Ms. O'Brien's doctors have security clearance to see her." She looked at her computer screen. "And your name is not on the list," she said. "I'm sorry." She smiled thinly. "I'm sure you understand that we need to do what's best for Ms. O'Brien. Unexpected visitors can set back her treatment, you know."

"I'm not unexpected," I said. "She's been asking for me. I'm her . . . her hero." When I said it out loud, I sounded like the biggest idiot in the world. I couldn't believe I'd said something so dumb. "I think she wants to see me," I added, trying to sound more confident. "She sent me these letters."

The receptionist laughed. "Oh, Mr. Black," she said. "Don't you know how many letters like that Sophie sends out each day?" She took her glasses off to wipe her eyes, as if this were the funniest thing in the world. Her name was on a brass nameplate on the table. MRS. REDDING, it said. I hated the way Mrs. Redding was laughing at me.

"But Sophie and I have a—" I didn't know what to call it. "A history," I said.

Suddenly Mrs. Redding's eyes got small. "Oh," she said. "You're *that* Jonah."

I couldn't believe it! The way she said it, it was like I was a well-known escaped convict.

"I'm what Jonah?" I said.

"Well, now," Mrs. Redding said, smirking at me. "I think we all know your history with Sophie, Jonah. Obviously, it would not be good for Sophie to see you at this time."

"How can it not be good?" I said, my voice rising. A door opened, and a very large guy with a shaved head came into the reception area and stood about ten feet away from me looking threatening. Mrs. Redding probably had some way of calling security, like a secret footswitch or something. It was kind of cool that she thought I was that much of a threat.

I took a breath and tried to calm down so Mr. Clean wouldn't grab me by the scruff of the neck and throw me out the door. "Could you just tell me," I said, "who I would talk to in order to be given security clearance to speak with Sophie?"

"That would be Dr. Margano," said Mrs. Redding.

"Well, may I speak with him, please?"

"I'm afraid he's not in at the moment," she

——■——

said, with a kind of smile of victory. "But if I were you, I wouldn't waste my time. Your name is specified here in our records as someone to keep away from Ms. O'Brien. I'm sure you understand. Now, is there anything else I can do for you today?"

"But what did I do?" I said. Mr. Clean started walking toward me. "I didn't do anything."

"Jonah," sighed Mrs. Redding, as if she had lost all patience with me. "If it weren't for you, Sophie wouldn't be here."

"That's a lie," I said. "Who told you that?"

Mr. Clean grabbed me under the arms. I felt like a nut in a pair of crackers. "Let's go, kid," he said.

I imagined Mr. Clean pulling my head off like the cork from a wine bottle. I decided to cooperate.

A minute later I was back in my father's Mercedes, which was technically a stolen car. Not that I told anyone that.

When I got back to Dad's house, everything was very quiet. I guess no one even noticed I was gone. I walked into the front hallway and looked at the chandelier hanging down overhead, and the long staircase in front of me.

"Hello?" I called. There was no response.

I walked up the stairs, past the small office off the landing where Dad pays his bills, up to the second floor, with Tiffany and Dad's room to the right, and on

—■—

the other side of the hall, their huge bathroom with the Jacuzzi and beyond that the big room with the fireplace that Dad calls the library. I don't know what they need a library for. Dad only reads newspapers and trashy best-sellers, and Tiffany only reads magazines.

I figured dad was probably in the library doing the Saturday crossword puzzle, which was his usual routine—but instead of going in there I got stuck at the entrance to the guest room, where Honey was sleeping. There were cans of paint on the floor and swatches of wallpaper and fabric tacked to the wall. The name of the paint color was Candy Girl. One of the wallpaper swatches was printed with rose petals. Everything was dark pink. It was like Honey's decorating nightmare.

"Which one do you think she'd like?" Tiffany asked from behind me. I almost jumped onto the ceiling.

"What?" I said. "Who?"

Tiffany was wearing a flowy lavender dress made of hemp-like fabric. It was hemmed with purple velvet ribbon. I was amazed how small she was. She can't weigh more than a hundred pounds, and at least ten pounds of that is in her hair, which is really long and bleached white-blond. Anyway, if Tiffany was pregnant, her baby was really small

—— ■ ——

because Tiffany weighed less pregnant than most little girls do when they're ten years old.

"Your sister, Honor. Do you think she'd like these colors?" Tiffany asked. "I'm redecorating."

I smiled. "You know, everybody calls her Honey," I said.

"I prefer not to," Tiffany said.

I wanted to smack her. What kind of thing is that to say, *I prefer not to*? If Honey wanted to be called Honey, then that's what Tiffany should call her.

"In any case," Tiffany said. "Do you think it will be to her liking?"

I forced myself not to laugh. Everything Tiffany had chosen had so little in common with Honey. But I had to give Tiffany credit for trying to connect to Honey on some level.

Then I thought, wait a minute, Tiffany doesn't want to connect to Honey. If she did, she'd have asked Honey what she wanted this room to look like before redecorating it. Maybe she'd even picked stuff that would make Honey sick to her stomach on purpose. She knew that Honey would rather leave than spend the night in there.

"Well, I don't know," I said. "I mean, they're pretty and all. Honey's just not really a pink person. But I'm sure she'll appreciate the time you've put into this."

—■—

"Do you think so? You really think your sister appreciates my time and effort?" she asked.

I nodded.

"Well," Tiffany said, shrugging this off as if what we were talking about wasn't really important. "We need not worry what Honor thinks."

"We need not?" I said.

"No," said Tiffany. She reached up with one hand to lift her mass of blond hair.

"Honor has fled the premises," Tiffany said, letting her hair fall again.

"Fled?" I said.

"Yes," Tiffany said. "She has continued on to Harvard." And with that she snatched the swatch of pink rose petal wallpaper off the wall and left the room. I bet she called in the order to the decorating store, now that she knows Honey isn't a pink person.

I headed into the library. Dad was in there, doing the crossword puzzle, just as I thought.

"Hello, Jonah," he said, taking off his glasses and smiling tightly. Again I noticed the lines on his face. I wonder why Tiffany doesn't give him some age cream for his face. I bet she has lots of creams.

We talked for a little bit. He said Honey would be back from Harvard in a couple of days. Fortunately, he didn't raise the issue of my stealing the car. I

———■———

realize now, Dad must not remember that I don't have my license.

Then, out of the blue, he asked, "Do you resent me, Jonah?"

"Do I resent you?" I repeated.

"Yes," Dad said. "Do you?"

I didn't know what to tell him. I mean, I don't really resent Dad. And if I do, the main thing I resent him for is asking me questions like do I resent him.

"No, not really. I mean, I'm sad about the divorce and everything. . . . And we don't really talk much," I told him. "But I don't sit around resenting you."

"I resented my old man," Dad said, shaking his head. "That stubborn old bastard." He didn't sound angry. The way he said it actually sounded like he was thinking of my grandfather fondly.

I took a deep breath. "If you want to know the truth, I feel like you've kind of moved on, Dad. Like, Honey and I are some part of your life you don't really want to deal with anymore."

"That's not true," Dad said. "How can you think that? You know I love you and Honor. You're my children."

"Well." I wasn't quite sure what to tell him. I didn't have much practice sharing my feelings with Dad. "Maybe you should show it more often."

Dad sighed. He sounded annoyed. "I show it as best I can."

"I think Honey especially would appreciate it if you were more interested in her," I added. I was on a roll.

"I *am* interested in her. I'm proud of her. I'm proud of both of you, Jonah!" He practically shouted this at me, as if saying it loud would make it true.

"Well, it doesn't feel like it sometimes," I said.

Dad put his paper down and sighed. "You should know that your sister and I had a bit of a spat today before she left. Your sister and I and Tiffany."

"A spat?"

"Yes. A regular to-do. And I have to say Jonah, I don't appreciate that kind of disruption right now. Tiffany is entitled to a little tranquility in her own house, don't you think?"

"Yes, I understand that," I said. I wondered what they'd fought about.

"I'm worried about Honor," Dad said. "I think she must be associating with a bad crowd. She hardly seems like the little girl I knew."

I wanted to say something in Honey's defense, but I couldn't think of exactly what to say. Dad hasn't exactly made the effort to get to know Honey in her current incarnation. But even if he did, he

—■—

wouldn't get it. Dad likes things straightforward and simple. Honey's too much for him.

"Tiffany in particular is rather upset about Honor's behavior," Dad said. "The two of them had a regular set-to, Jonah. Words were exchanged."

"I'm sorry to hear that," I said. I wondered what kind of words they had exchanged. Honey knows a lot of them.

"I am hoping things will improve upon her return," Dad said. "I am hoping Harvard will exert a positive influence on her. Do you think it will?"

I lied. And I think he knew I was lying, but it was what he needed to hear. "Absolutely," I said. "I bet when Honey gets back, you won't even recognize her."

"Good," said Dad.

Feb. 1

Weird morning. So far I've just been lying around, watching television and reading the paper. I'm not really sure what to do with myself.

About an hour ago, Dad and Tiffany went out to brunch. On their way out I said to Dad, all casual-like, "Is it okay if I take the car later?"

Dad said, "Of course, Jonah," and just kept on moving. I can't believe he's completely forgotten about my little accident last spring. It's kind of a hard thing to forget. Tiffany didn't say anything to me, but before she left she picked up Cuddles and kissed him on the mouth. I wonder how that makes Dad feel.

On their way back from brunch, they're going to stop at this place called Space which is some sort of high-end home-decorating store. Tiffany's decided she's going to redo my room.

I thought she'd already had her way with my room. Obviously she wanted to make it even weirder than it already was. "Actually," I said. "The room is really fine the way it is," I said.

"I think not," Tiffany said.

"You better stand aside, son," Dad said, winking at me. "When Tiffany decides she's going to redecorate, there's no stopping her!" He put his arm around her, like this was Tiffany's most endearing quality.

I thought about what she's planning to do to Honey's room. "No, really," I said. "I like it. It's fine."

"It is *not* fine," Tiffany said, rolling her eyes. *"Honestly."*

It seemed weird that she didn't care that I asked her to leave the room alone. It was my room, after all.

"I'm just saying you don't have to do anything special up there," I said.

Tiffany drew her lips into a thin line and then attempted a smile. "Oh, Jonah, I think you might be surprised. You might like the improvement." She buttoned her coat and slung her purse over her arm. "We have to go now. I'm famished."

Dad just shook his head and winked at me again. "What did I tell you, son?" he said. "You don't

---

want to get between Tiffany and her decorating."

Then they went out to the garage and I watched Dad help Tiffany into the passenger seat of her new white Volvo. He backed out of the driveway very cautiously. I guess with a baby on board he's being extra careful.

I guess Dad's really in love with Tiffany. And everything she does that I think is horrible and annoying, Dad thinks is adorable and wonderful. It's like he's joined a cult. The cult of Tiffany, Cuddles, and rose petal wallpaper.

Is that how I am about Sophie? I mean, I think she's wonderful, but would my friends be annoyed by her if they met her? I'm not sure.

(Later.)

Since Tiffany and Dad took the Volvo, I decided to have an adventure in the Mercedes. I drove over to Masthead.

Sunday is always pretty low key there, because it's the day people actually do homework, at least starting in the afternoon. During the day people hang out, go to the gym, lie around the dorms. I wasn't quite sure what I wanted to do once I got over there, but I had to go.

As I drove there, I started imagining what it

———■———

would be like if I'd never been kicked out of school. I'd still be going to Masthead and living my life up here. The doors to the gym swing open and Sophie and I walk out into the winter air, hand in hand. Our breath gathers in clouds in the air, and we can feel the warmth of each others' hands through our gloves. Sophie leans her head into my chest and kisses me and I put my arm around her waist on top of her long blue coat. . . . In our hands are our acceptance letters from the University of Pennsylvania. We're going to live together, off campus, in a cool apartment on South Street. I reach down into my pocket and there is the small velvet box I've been carrying around for a long time. I stop walking and pull it out of my pocket. Sophie knows what is about to happen, but happy tears of love and surprise shine in her eyes. "Oh, Jonah," she cries. I pop open the box and the diamond glitters in the winter sun. "Sophie," I say, and I get down on one knee. I can feel the snow seeping into my pant leg where I'm kneeling. *Sophie.*

But I knew as I pulled into the gates of Masthead that I wouldn't see Sophie there.

"Jesus," I said out loud as I parked in front of Auburn Hall. I pulled the keys out of the ignition and sat there for a moment, looking up at the gray

---

Victorian building and the teachers' offices behind each window.

Then Dean Stubbs walked by and my heart started beating double-time in my chest. Of all the people to see first, I had to see the guy whose car I'd totaled. Dean Stubbs walked over to the faculty spots and got into his brand-new Peugeot. He started the engine, put on a pair of mirrored shades, and pulled out.

"Jesus," I said again. "I have to get out of here." But I didn't go anywhere. I just sat in the car, feeling like a convict who'd dug his way out of prison. And I knew I was going to have to get out of the car and walk around if I wanted to get whatever it was I wanted out of being there. So I did.

I pulled the collar of my coat up around my neck, and I pulled my wool hat down around my ears. It was the coat I'd worn all last year at Masthead, so it wasn't like I was very well disguised. It's funny, I don't even have a warm coat like that in Florida. I'd found it in Dad's closet. Anyway, I got out of the Mercedes, which was pulled up by a sign that said VISITORS' PARKING, and I started walking around.

Inside my head a little voice kept asking, *Why are you here, Jonah? What are you looking for?*

I knew I was taking a big risk, because when

---

they kicked me out of Masthead they'd specifically said I was never allowed on campus again. They didn't say what they'd do to me, but I wouldn't have been all that surprised if they called the cops and threw me in jail. Everybody knows the security guys at Masthead are seriously uptight. They drive around in little blue vans, wearing uniforms and carrying walkie-talkies and heavy flashlights, looking for disturbances or suspicious characters, like me.

I opened the door to Auburn Hall and started walking through the hallways. Because it's Sunday, it was nearly deserted, although the lights were still on. It felt like a ship that had been abandoned before it sank. I wondered if I went down into the basement if I'd see water leaking in.

I went upstairs.

Above me, from the fourth floor music practice rooms, I could hear someone playing the violin. It was probably Linda Sayewich. Linda was this kind of small, mousy, quiet girl who totally blossomed when she played violin. Her eyes closed and you could see them moving around behind her eyelids, like she was dancing in the world of her head in time to the amazing music she was playing.

I think the piece she was playing was called "In

——■——

the Hall of the Mountain King." I recognized it from music class. It's a pretty spooky song.

I walked by the old art studio and stopped. There were a few easels scattered around a pedestal in the center of the room. I went over and looked at the paintings in the easels. They were all of this old man, draped in a sheet like a Roman emperor. He made me think of Pops. Pops would get a kick out of standing in the middle of a room wearing nothing but a sheet while everybody painted him.

There was a faint sniffling sound from the corner, and I look over and there she is, working on her oil painting. There's a blob of yellow paint in her hair. She has her back turned to me. I can't believe she's sitting there—it's like she's waiting for me. I walk up behind her, and for a moment I just stand there and look at the painting. It's the portrait of the girl on the cliff, about to jump, the one that first got my attention before I even knew her. She's painted in the ocean. The waves are crashing against the rocks.

I'm so happy she's back. She must have gotten out of Maggins somehow. And now she's back where she always loved to be, sitting in the art studio, working on her painting. I'd forgotten what a good artist she was, how pretty her hair is, how perfect she is. I lean forward to kiss her on the neck. I will

---

wait until she knows it's me, then I'll softly whisper her name—*Sophie!*

At that second, the girl looked up with frightened eyes and said, "What are you doing?"

I just stood there. I felt so embarrassed.

The girl held up her paintbrush as if to stab me with it. The end was covered in yellow paint. The painting she was working on wasn't of a cliff, it was just a still life, some yellow flowers on a table.

"I'm sorry," I said, and backed away. "I thought you were somebody else."

I turned and headed out of there, hoping she wouldn't think I was some psycho stalker. Behind me I heard the girl following me out into the hall.

"Jonah?" she called. "Are you Jonah Black?"

I ran down the stairs and went back outside. I should have gone straight back to the car and home to Dad's. But I never do what I'm supposed to.

I still had this feeling that I hadn't found what I'd come looking for, even though I didn't know what I was looking for. I walked through the quad, past the sundial in the courtyard. Snow was starting to fall, and it gathered on the collar of my coat. The face of the sundial was covered up with snow, but underneath the snow I knew were engraved the words: GROW OLD ALONG WITH ME. THE BEST IS YET TO BE.

I walked through the courtyard to the gym and

went inside. In the main foyer, in huge glass cases, were the hundreds of awards and trophies that Masthead has won since 1884. I paused by the shelf holding the ones for the swim team.

There on a plaque at the bottom of a large golden cup was the inscription: JONAH BLACK, INTERAC DIVING CHAMPION. It was from last year.

I couldn't believe it. I remember winning that meet for Masthead, but I didn't know there was a trophy for it. They must have handed it out on Ivy Day—which was the day before graduation. By that time, I'd already been expelled.

I wondered if it had bugged the headmaster that the Interac Conference had awarded this trophy to me when I wasn't even one of Masthead's students anymore. That made me feel good, like I had something on them.

I walked down the stairs and onto the viewing balcony above the pool. The smell of the pool reminded me of the old practices. The sound of the coach's whistle. I could almost feel my eyes stinging with chlorine.

Somebody was swimming in the pool, a really scrawny-looking guy with moles all over his back. He was probably a ninth grader.

I wondered if the girl who had seen me in the art studio had called security. I had a feeling it was

---

just a matter of time before someone caught me and asked me to leave.

I left the gym and went outside. The snow was coming down harder now. I walked across the quad. Every single thing I looked at sent me into this spiral, back in time. Like, over there I was sitting with Betsy Donnelly, eating potato chips before German class. Over there I was playing Frisbee with Brian Wittenberg and Mr. Franko. Over here I was running in my gym shorts, doing the two-mile loop on the off-season. And over there, and there, and there—everywhere I looked—was Sophie, walking in her gray skirt, her hair shining in the sun.

The next thing I knew, I was standing in front of Whittaker. My old dorm.

I could hear music playing inside, even with all the windows closed. People were going in and out. I looked up at the third window on the second floor, and there was Sophie looking out at me. At first she doesn't recognize me, but then she remembers. She opens the window and leans out.

I want to call out, *Careful Sophie, don't lean too far.* But Sophie leans even farther. I'm scared she's going to fall. I walk closer and open my arms to catch her. Sophie leaps out into the winter air and falls very slowly, like her skirt is a kind of parachute. All I can do is stand there with my arms out, waiting to catch her.

—— ▪ ——

Someone pushed open the doors of Whittaker and lumbered down the steps. It was my old roommate, Sullivan the Giant.

He stomped past me in the snow and headed across the quad. He seemed even bigger than before, and he has a buzz cut now, from spending last semester at Valley Forge Military Academy. He even moved in this kind of robotic, murderous way, like he was still a soldier. Just looking at him sort of scared me, but I followed him anyway.

The snow was falling heavily now, and I watched the flakes gather on the shoulders of his black wool coat. They melted as they hit his hair, and I could almost imagine a soft *tsssss* sound as the cold flakes hit his hot head.

As I followed Sullivan I remembered lying in our dorm room, listening to him boast about all the girls he'd taken advantage of. How he'd gotten information from his trustee father about each girl and blackmailed them, one by one, into doing what he wanted. One day in the spring, Sophie O'Brien was next on his list. I could still hear his disgusting voice describing what he was going to do to my Sophie once he got her naked at the Beeswax Inn. I remembered lying there in my bed, staring at the ceiling, thinking, *I have to stop him.*

I knew that he was back at Masthead because

— ■ —

Betsy had told me. And now that I'd seen him, I realized what I had come to Masthead to do.

I was going to punch this lowlife loser's lights out and tell him to stay away from Sophie.

It was actually pretty funny to even think about punching someone since I've never punched anybody in my life. And given Sullivan's size and the fact that he's never liked me anyway—he wasn't going to take it well. I would punch him once and then I would get flattened. But as long as I could punch him the one time, I didn't care what happened after that.

Sullivan stopped by the pay phone in the quad and picked it up. I started toward him, my hands balling into fists.

Then someone grabbed me by the elbow of my bad arm and put a hand very firmly on my back and said, "Let's keep walking, Mr. Black." It was a woman.

I turned to find a woman cop with mirrored shades and a white hat shoving me toward the parking lot. Sullivan looked over at me, and I'm pretty sure he recognized me. The last time Sullivan had seen me, I'd been in the back of a cop car, driving away into the night. He gave me the thumbs-up sign, like getting arrested was my big aim in life, and now I'd done it again.

"Which car is yours, Mr. Black?" said the security guard. I couldn't even talk. I pointed at Dad's Mercedes. "Get in," she said. I got into the car, and she walked around and opened the passenger side door and sat down next to me.

"Drive," she said.

"You want me to—"

"Drive," she said again.

I put the car in gear and I pulled out onto Lancaster Pike. I didn't cut the turn very well, though, and I just narrowly missed this fire hydrant on the corner. The whole car lurched as we bumped over the curb.

"Jesus, Jonah," the guard said. "Your driving hasn't gotten any better."

I looked over at her, and she was kind of grinning at me. Then she took off her white hat and sunglasses.

"Betsy," I said. "Whoa. I thought you were a cop. I thought you were going to arrest me!"

"I should," she said. "Are you out of your mind, sneaking around campus? That girl you saw in the art room called Security. Lucky for you, I was the one who got the call."

"Since when are you working for campus security?"

"Since my father got sick and we can't afford Masthead tuition anymore without work-study."

—■—

Betsy looked great. There was a wisp of brown hair falling down on the right side of her face. She had a blue vein on her throat, too, that I'd never seen. It was very cool and confident-looking, pulsing under her white skin. Why had I never noticed that before?

"Wow. I'm sorry."

"It's all right, Jonah. I'm okay. But I want to know what the hell you're doing at Masthead. What the hell you're doing in Pennsylvania."

I kept driving down the turnpike, very slowly, through the snow. I thought about the road up here, with Honey at the Museum for Retired Ventriloquists' Dummies and the World's Largest Monopoly Board. And about Sophie locked up at Maggins. How was I ever going to get in to see her? In the glow from headlights of an oncoming car I could see Sophie's face, pleading, *Help me, Jonah.*

"Oh, no," Betsy said. "You're not."

"I'm not what?" I said, all innocent.

"You're not up here to get Sophie O'Brien out of Maggins, are you?" Betsy asked.

I just shrugged. And then I blushed deep red.

"Stop the car," Betsy said. "Now." That vein on her throat pulsed again.

I pulled over. Cars on the Lancaster Pike honked at me.

——■——

Betsy got out a pair of handcuffs and snapped one cuff around my wrist. Then she snapped the other one around the wheel. She turned on the radio and turned the dial around. The fundamentalist Christian station came on. She turned the volume way up.

Then she opened the door and got out of the car. "I'm leaving," Betsy said.

"You're what?"

"You heard me." She put her white hat and sunglasses back on. They made her look pretty dangerous and sexy. "I should have arrested you," she said. "I should have hit you in the head with my flashlight."

"Why?" I said. "What did I do?"

"Because," Betsy said. "Practically a year has gone by, and you haven't learned a damned thing."

And then she walked down the sidewalk, back toward Masthead, leaving me handcuffed to the steering wheel of the car, the traffic snarling around me. A preacher on the radio was sermonizing. "Repent," he said. "Repent."

Feb. 2, 5 P.M.

Okay, it's the next day, but I still need to catch up on yesterday. There's a lot more to tell, not only about yesterday but today, too.

So I sat there on the Lancaster Pike with cars honking at me while I kind of tried to get the car back in gear, but I couldn't really drive with the handcuffs. It wouldn't have been safe. Fortunately Betsy came back after about ten minutes and unlocked me.

"Okay, Jonah," she said. "Let's go to Dunkin' Donuts."

I guess Betsy was being funny. Like, now that she's a campus cop she has to eat doughnuts. Anyway, I drove to Dunkin' Donuts and we got out of the car and went inside and sat at the counter. I

———■———

sat there rubbing my bad arm, which still hurt from when Betsy had grabbed it.

I got a Boston Kreme. Betsy got a plain cruller. We both got coffee, even though I don't really drink it. I poured in three sugars and lots of cream. Betsy laughed at me.

"I'm sorry I handcuffed you," Betsy said. "I guess that was kind of mean."

She took her hat off of her head and pulled out her ponytail elastic. All her hair spilled down her back and around her face. It made her look a lot less intimidating. That vein on her throat wasn't pulsing anymore, either. Betsy put the hat down on the counter in front of her.

"I don't know," I said. "You seemed like you enjoyed it."

"I just get tired of you being so obsessed with Sophie. You know she's a total loon, right?"

I picked at my doughnut. "Yeah, I know."

"Well, I don't think you do. All sorts of stuff has happened in the last month or two," she said.

I wasn't sure I wanted to hear about it, but I waited for her to tell me more.

Betsy took a big sip of her coffee.

"Well, the rumor is Sophie isn't going to be in Maggins much longer," she explained. "Her father's coming down from Maine to take her home."

—■—

I thought about this. Maybe it would be a good thing, for Sophie to head home for a while and relax. But if she went all the way back to Maine, I'd be losing her forever. At least, that's what it felt like.

"But here's the scary thing," Betsy said. "Sullivan's gotten his father to talk the doctors into keeping Sophie in Maggins a little longer. They won't discharge her until after he's had a chance to see her."

I stopped breathing for a second. "Wait," I said. "Until *who* gets a chance to see her?"

"Sullivan," she said, looking down at her hands.

I stared into my full coffee cup.

"I don't know how to tell you this, Jonah, but she's been talking to Sullivan again."

I felt like my heart got shot out of my chest and straight into my coffee. I thought about the big thumbs-up Sullivan had given me when Betsy hauled me off the Masthead campus.

"What do mean?" I said.

"Well, maybe I shouldn't call it talking. I mean, nobody can really talk to her. But Sullivan's been e-mailing her all these hot messages, and she's been e-mailing him back."

I felt blood heating up my cheeks. What could Sophie be thinking? Sullivan is the guy I saved her from, the guy I sacrificed everything to keep her away from. And now she's swapping "hot" e-mails

—■—

with him? It made me sick just thinking about it.

"How do you know all this?" I asked.

"Because Sophie told me. We've been staying in touch," Betsy said. "And you might as well know, she's told him that she loves him. She's told him she's waiting for him."

Now I really felt sick.

"I don't believe you," I said, almost shouting. "She told me she loves *me*. She's waiting for *me*."

Betsy shrugged. "I'm just telling you what Sophie told me. But it's hard to believe anything she says. She's a real wacko, Jonah."

"Oh, my God," I said. "I've got to—"

"No, you don't," said Betsy, grabbing my sore wrist. "You know what you have to do, Jonah? Forget about her."

"I can't," I said, trying to pull away.

"Yes, you can," Betsy said. She slid her hand over mine and looked into my eyes. She had freckles on her nose and beautiful, light brown eyes. "You need to move on," she said. "You know?"

She moves toward me and we kiss. She unbuttons the top of her security uniform and it falls onto the floor of the Dunkin' Donuts. She isn't wearing a bra underneath, just these pink panties, and a weird kind of sparkling belt that goes all the way around her belly.

"Jonah," Sophie says. "I've been waiting for you."

I lean forward to kiss her again and I know that this time, Sophie is not going to run away, and she is not going to cry. We are going to be together forever, just like we were always meant to be.

"Damn," Betsy said, pulling her hand away and putting her hat back on. "You really are hopeless, aren't you?"

"Wait," I said. "I'm not hopeless." But Betsy was already back on her feet.

"Could have fooled me," she said.

"I'm sorry," I said. "It's just that if I don't look out for Sophie, I don't know who's going to, you know?"

Betsy looked at me hard, and sighed. She sat back down again. "Oh, Jonah," she said. "You really are like, the last romantic in the world, aren't you?"

"I don't know," I said. I took a bite of my doughnut. It was dry.

"You are. I'm sorry I handcuffed you. I get frustrated." Betsy fiddled with her sunglasses. "I mean, there are a lot of girls out there who would love to be with you—who wish you would let go of Sophie and notice them for a change, you know? You're so hung up on this one girl who's like, a black hole. And you know she's only going to screw with your head again, right?"

I nodded. "Yeah," I said. "Probably."

"Okay," she said. "Well, I should go and leave you alone. But there's one more thing you should know. I think Sullivan is going to get clearance to go see Sophie. The doctors at Maggins think that seeing Sullivan may help her with her trouble."

"Her trouble?" I said. "What is her trouble?"

"Jonah," Betsy said, furrowing her freckly forehead. "They think her trouble is you."

(Later.)

Well, it's late now, but I might as well write down the last major thing that happened today.

Honey came back from Harvard, where she apparently scared the hell out of everyone and made them regret they ever let her in. I think her plan was to make sure she got a single room for the fall, which looks pretty definite now. From the way she says she acted when she was up there I think if they gave Honey a roommate they could count on that roommate transferring to someplace else before the end of the first week of classes.

The important news, though, is that Honey didn't come back from Harvard alone.

Honey brought this guy Maximillian back with her. Max, as Honey calls him, has his head completely shaved on the sides, but it's really long on top and pulled back into a ponytail. He has something which you can't really call a beard—it's like a thin line between his lower lip and his chin. And he has these very sparkly, jovial eyes. His clothes are all covered with paint—even his shoes.

Max is in some band called Severed, which Honey has heard of. When I told her I didn't know anything about Severed, she looked at me like I was stupid. "It's okay," Max said. "Not everybody's into it. There's no rule that you have to have heard of anything."

"He should have heard about Severed, though," Honey insisted. "You guys rock."

"It doesn't matter," said Max. "The world is big."

The thing is, I think I actually like Max. There's something incredibly sweet and gentle about him, even if half his head is shaved and he is in a band called Severed. He asked me lots of questions, too, as if he was really interested.

We were in Honey's bedroom, which—for the time being—is still all beige. Honey saw the cans of pink paint and the pink wallpaper samples and said, "Ha!" But Max didn't seem to mind them. He had changed into these black-and-white striped pajamas, which were covered in green paint, while Honey tinkered with her robot.

"Do you think of yourself as an angry person, Jonah?" Max asked me.

—■—

"Well, no," I said. "I mean there are things I'm mad about, but I'm not exactly angry, if that makes any sense."

"I understand that completely," said Max.

"It wouldn't be a bad thing if you got mad once in a while, Jonah," Honey said. "It's good for you." She was twisting a screw in the guts of the robot.

"Bzzzzrp," the robot said. *"Znnnnnt."*

"Hey, Honor," Max said. "Let me do that."

Honey gave him the screwdriver.

"See, the thing about black metal music," Max explained, as he fiddled with the robot, "is its deep anger. Its aggression. Most of the people who listen to it are pretty angry. They've spent their whole lives feeling like they're different, like nobody gets it, like they're just totally outside the workings of the planet. Then they plug in to Mudvayne or Cradle of Filth, or, God Deathrone, Mushmouth, or Korn, or—

"Or Severed," Honey said.

"And it's like somebody is actually listening to them." Suddenly Max's face lit up. The robot made this humming sound. "There you go, Honor," he said. "You had a bad capacitor." He started typing things in on this little keyboard, and watching a small monitor. "Yes, yes, yes," he said. He grabbed the phone off the table and pulled the cord out of the bottom and plugged it into the robot. "Ooh, wee!"

"Max performs as Scabbaxx," Honey said.

I just looked at her blankly. "His father was the original Scabbaxx?" she said. "In Poison Squirrels?"

I nodded. "Ah, right. *That* Scabbaxx."

I looked at Max. His lips were moving softly as he typed on the keyboard. "So your dad was a musician, too?" I asked him.

"Yup," said Honey. She was looking at Max with an expression of awe and admiration that I've never seen on her face before. That's when I realized. Honey's in love!

"So how was Harvard?" I asked her.

"Harvard sucks, man!" she shouted. "I can't wait to go there."

"Yeah?" I said. "I thought you said everyone there was going to be a loser."

"Yeah, mostly," she said.

Electra said, "It is a wise man who knows better than to throw his pearls before swine."

"Hey, Honor," Max said. "What does that mean? Pearls before swine?"

"It's a metaphor, Max," Honey said. "It means if you have something valuable you don't throw it in the path of somebody who can't appreciate it."

"I know what it means, Sweetstuff," said Max. "I'm just not into the verbiage."

"It's from Matthew. Matthew 7:5," said Honey.

"It's Matthew 7:6," countered Max. "I still don't like the verbiage."

"You guys know the Bible?" I said. I don't know why it should have surprised me.

"Old Testament, New Testament," Max said. "Koran. Tibetan Book of the Dead. I've read them all."

"The Tibetan Book of the Dead sucks," Honey said.

"No way, Honor," he said. "Did you read it in translation?"

"What, you read the original?" Honey said, her eyes all dreamy.

Max shrugged. "I like Sanskrit."

Honey just smiled at him. I couldn't believe it. It was like they were made for each other.

Max typed some more, and then hit Enter. "Okay, now we just have to wait a bit to see if it works." He got up and went over to a backpack on the floor that had a skull and crossbones on it. He reached in and pulled something out. "There's something I want you to have, Little Master," he said. He walked over, and put something heavy in my hand. "Take this," he said. "You may need it."

I opened my hand. It was a metal ball. It felt like it was made of lead. "What's this?" I said.

"What's it look like?" said Max.

Honey nodded. "Nice one, Max," she said.

I just stared at the ball.

———■———

"It's for luck," Max told me, his face serious. "You might want to have it. Okay?"

"Okay," I said. I put the ball in my pocket.

"Atta boy!" the robot said.

Max's face lit up and he smiled. "We're in!" he shouted.

"In where?" I said.

Max typed some more stuff into Electra's keyboard. "You're clear, Little Master," he said.

"What do you mean, I'm clear?" I said.

"Show up at this Maggins place, tomorrow at ten-thirty A.M. Tell 'em you're Mr. Smith-Smith. They'll let you take that girl Sophie out for a ride in your car. You've got security clearance for an hour and a half."

"What? How did you do that?"

"It's a snap, Little Master," said Max. "Honor built herself a real smart robot."

Honey blushed.

"So I'm—? I can—?" I stammered. I couldn't believe I actually had clearance to see Sophie. Tomorrow morning, in the flesh.

"You are," Max said. "And you can."

"Wow," I said. I could barely breathe.

"Max goes to Harvard," Honey said, beaming. I've never seen her look so happy before.

I nodded. "Uh-huh." I guess Honey doesn't mind the idea of Harvard so much anymore.

"Uh-oh, wait a minute," Max said, looking at the monitor again. "Little Master, you know anybody named Sullivan?"

I felt the color drain from my face. I nodded.

"Well he's coming in right after you," Max said. "He's scheduled to see her at noon. So you do whatever you need to do before twelve, okay? 'Cause this guy Sullivan is the next one in line, after you bring her back."

Then I said something that surprised me. I didn't know I'd decided it until I said it.

"I'm not bringing her back," I said.

Max got up and put his arm around Honey.

"Good night, Little Master," Max and Honey said in unison.

"Good night," I said, and walked out of Honey's bedroom, turning the heavy metal ball over and over in my hand.

And now I'm lying in bed, writing this. Honey and Maximillian are "asleep" across the hall. Tiffany and Cuddles are locked in their bedroom. Dad is drinking gin in the library.

And Sophie is in her room at Maggins, with no idea that I'm about to come save her again, hopefully for the last time.

Feb. 3

I'm just about to head over to Maggins to see Sophie. I'm wearing a white shirt and a tie that I wore last year when I was a Masthead student.

There is this one big hole in Honey and Max's plan, which is that Mrs. Redding is probably going to be at the front desk again. I don't think the tie is going to disguise me very well. Anyway, I'm going to go over there and see who's at reception. If it's someone other than Mrs. Redding, I'll walk in there and say I'm Mr. Smith-Smith. If it's Mrs. Redding, I think I'll have to go and buy a disguise. There is actually a store in Bryn Mawr that sells costumes, so this isn't out of the question. I could wear a gorilla head. Or I could dress up like a guy who really knows what he's doing, somebody

———■———

without any problems. That way they'd never recognize me.

Plus, I got this e-mail this morning:

To: JBlack94710
From: Northgirl999

Jonah, did you see Sophie yet? Everyone at Don Shula thinks you had to go back to Pennsylvania because your murder trial started. Your friend Thorne Wood says you're accused of manslaughter, which I think he made up because he thinks girls will think it's sexy. Are you really friends with him? He seems like such an idiot if you ask me. Anyway, I am worried about you, Jonah. Molly Beale told Elanor Brubaker that she had the greatest sex of her life with you. That isn't true either, is it? My guess is you broke up with her. I really like Molly but I can see how you'd get tired of her. She's pretty intense. Speaking of breaking up, I broke up with the guy I was seeing so now I am single again and totally horny.

Maybe when you come back to Florida I will tell you who I am. Assuming you do come back to Florida.

My prediction is, you come back to Florida and you and I finally start to see each other. Once you realize that you don't want Sophie, that is.

Anyway, you still have to guess who I am first.

—— ■ ——

Okay, I'm out of here. I'm going to see Sophie. Well, first I'm going to stop at the Wawa to get condoms. I know it's kind of presumptuous of me, but I just feel like I should have some. I can't believe this is happening.

—■—

Feb. 5

Two days later. I can't believe I haven't had the time to write in my journal, but it makes sense. Now I've got all the time in the world. I wish I didn't, but I do.

It's going to take a while for me to get down everything that's happened over the last couple of days. But I'll start where I left off and see how far I get before my hand gets tired.

I drove over to Maggins, and it looked even creepier to me than it did the first time. Maybe it was the snow. It seems like people would get worse after spending time there, not better. I parked Dad's Mercedes and walked up the front steps. The sky was gray and it felt like it was about to start snowing again. I put my hands in my pockets because I didn't have any gloves.

—■—

And there in the pocket of my jacket was Max's metal ball. It felt cold, but I squeezed it so hard it warmed up right away

I pushed open the door and walked into the front hallway.

To my relief, it wasn't Mrs. Redding at the desk, although I did take the precaution of stealing Dad's reading glasses before I left the house. I was kind of hoping they would make me look older, and more like a Mr. Smith-Smith. The reading glasses magnified my eyes so that they looked huge. I don't know what the woman at the desk thought of me. She was younger than Mrs. Redding and she didn't have a nameplate.

I cleared my throat and said the line I'd rehearsed all the way over there in the car. "Hello, my name is Mr. Smith-Smith. I believe I'm cleared to take Sophie O'Brien out for a short excursion."

The woman looked up and seemed kind of panicked. She knocked a glass of water over on her desk.

"Oh, I'm sorry," she said. "I'm such an idiot."

"That's all right," I said.

"I'm just temping here. Their regular receptionist— Mrs.— what's her name?"

"Mrs. Redding," I said. I felt very well-informed, knowing the regular receptionist's name. It made me more credible.

—■—

"Yeah, well, she got a message from the police about an hour ago. Something about her house being on fire or something. She had to leave."

Thank you, Max, I thought to myself. No wonder he goes to Harvard.

The woman mopped up the water with some tissues. Then her fingertips hammered at her keyboard and she looked at her computer screen. After a moment she said, "Mm-hmm, that's fine. I have you right here. She needs to be back by noon."

"I understand," I said.

She gave me a visitor's badge that said SMITH-SMITH on it, and then she nodded toward the door and said, "Room 109. She's resting right now. I'm sure she's expecting you."

I walked through the door, into this kind of common room, and I suddenly realized the seriousness of what I was doing.

A bunch of girls my age were all sitting around, watching some soap opera on TV. Well, a couple of them were watching. One girl who had bandages all up and down her wrists was just sort of staring into space. Another girl sat on a radiator looking out the window. The window had bars on it. Two other girls were looking at the TV, crying, and holding hands. They were incredibly thin, like skeletons.

—■—

They all looked over at me as I walked through the common room. I felt like I was looking at puppies at the pound. In the distance, there was a girl wailing, and someone else, a nurse maybe, trying to calm her down.

Whoa, I thought, this place is for people who are really in trouble. I don't know why I was so shocked by this. I mean, Betsy told me Sophie was really troubled. I guess I just didn't want to believe it.

I passed by the room of this girl with huge gray eyes. She was writing in a red book entitled *My Diary*.

Then I reached room 109. Sophie was lying on her bed. "Oh, Jonah," she said, sitting up. "I was thinking it might be you."

Okay, I have to stop her for a sec. Honey wants to get a Frosty from Wendy's. I'm not even hungry, but I think I'll get some fries anyway.

(Still Feb. 5)

Okay, back to meeting Sophie at Maggins.

"Yeah, it's me," I said. "Hi, Sophie."

Sophie was wearing a pale pink T-shirt and white Capri pants, even though it's winter. I guess she didn't get out much. Her hair was longer and straighter than I remembered, and it hung loose

———▪———

on her shoulders. She wasn't wearing any makeup, just the little diamond studs in her ears that she always wore at Masthead. I gave her some earrings when I saw her in Orlando. I wonder if she ever wears them. There were big tired circles under her eyes, and, strangely, she was wearing glasses. She took these off when I came in. I could smell her shampoo and I remembered the smell—of daisies and sunlight. She smiled and the smile changed her whole face. A second before I'd thought she looked tired. Now all I could think was, *Wow, is she beautiful.*

Her room was very bare. There was a bed and an institutional-looking dresser and a small desk with two books on it: *The Great Gatsby* and *The Lord of the Rings.* There were lots of loose pieces of paper with her handwriting on them too. In the closet a few of her things were hanging on hangers. There was one yellow dress I remembered from Orlando.

"How are you, Sophie?" I asked.

"I didn't think they'd let you see me. They think you're the cause of all my problems," she said.

I sat down on the bed and took her hand.

"Is it okay that I came?" I said. "Really?"

"Jonah," she said. Then she leaned forward and kissed me.

Her kiss was soft and hot and needy. I felt like she was going to swallow me. She wrapped her arms around me and squeezed me a little tightly. She was hurting my bad arm.

"I knew you'd come," she said. "I knew it!" She glanced out the window. "Oh, not now," she said softly.

"What?"

"Nothing," Sophie said. "For a second I was thinking it was those helicopters again."

I remembered her saying something about helicopters when we were in the hotel room in Orlando together. It had kind of freaked me out then, too. My heart was beating quickly. If Sophie was in this place maybe she really was nuts. I was probably nuts myself for thinking I could ever help her.

"Don't think like that," Sophie said.

"Sorry," I said, although I didn't see how she could have known what I'd been thinking. "I've been worried about you," I said.

"Yeah, I'm worried about me, too," Sophie said, with an odd little smile. "I wasn't crazy when I got here, but I think I am now. The pills they give you . . ." Her eyes grew big and she pulled at the blanket on her bed. "You know, if you get cured they have to let you out, and then they lose

———■———

money. So they can't let you get better, no way, are you kidding?"

"Thanks for the e-mails," I said. "And the, uh—"

"Oh, no," Sophie said. She balled her fists and held them to her temples. "I can't believe I sent you that bird. I knew you'd think I was really insane when I did that. I felt so stupid. It was just that I found it and it seemed so sad, and so I mailed it to you and then I wanted to unmail it. I wanted to open up the mailbox but they wouldn't let me. They said the mailbox was like, the property of the goddamn government, like getting my package out of the mailbox was going to be some federal crime or something, and all I wanted was to get that box with the bird in it back and unmail it so you wouldn't think I was truly nuts. That's when they decided you were the cause of all my problems, Jonah. I didn't think they'd ever let me see you again."

"They don't know I'm me," I said, showing her my name tag.

"That's okay," she said. "They don't know I'm me, either."

I laughed, but Sophie wasn't joking.

"So what do you think, Jonah," she said. "Do you want to do it?"

"What, here? Now?" I said.

———■———

"Sure," said Sophie, and she reached down and pulled her shirt off. "This is my 'quiet time.' Nobody's going to bother us."

I looked at her and I thought, *Isn't this what I've always wanted?* But it wasn't. I didn't want to do it with Sophie inside a mental hospital during 'quiet time.' I wanted to get her out of there.

"Why don't we go somewhere else?" I said. "I have clearance to take you out for a couple of hours. Maybe we could talk?"

"Excellent," she said. She pulled her shirt back on and stood up and went over to her dresser. First she pulled her hair back in an elastic, then she pulled on some hiking boots without any socks, and then she got a big down coat out of the closet. And just like that we were ready to go.

"Why don't we go to that motel?" Sophie suggested. "You know, the one where you came to save me? I can't remember what it was called now." Her face turned all vacant.

"The Beeswax Inn?" I said.

"Yeah, yeah," Sophie said. "Let's head over to the Beeswax Inn and do it there!" She gave me another big hug.

I flinched. She was really hurting my arm.

What are you doing? I thought to myself. But I kept on doing it. It was like I couldn't wait to see what would happen next, even though I was the one making the decisions and calling the shots.

We walked back out through the common room and Sophie waved to the other girls, who were still sitting where they'd been sitting before. "Hey, I'm going on a field trip," she told them. "We're going to a motel room!"

The other girls just looked at her vacantly. It didn't even look like they were all that envious. They really scared me. I wish I could have helped them all.

(Later.)

Okay. So we got in the car. I drove down City Line toward the Beeswax Inn. Sophie looked out the window for a while and then said, "Wow, the world just keeps on going, doesn't it?"

I just said, "Yeah." I looked at her and tried to feel reassured, but I didn't. "I'm glad you're okay, Sophie," I said, as if saying it would actually make her okay.

Sophie didn't say anything for a while, then she turned to me and there were tears on her cheeks.

"Who said I was okay?" she said.

We drove past this fancy hotel on City Line

called The Morgan. When I was a student at Masthead, they'd still been building it. Now it was having its grand opening. There were flags flapping on flagpoles, and bunting hanging from the front awning.

"My Daddy's staying there," Sophie said, as if it was no big deal.

"Your dad?" I said. "He's here?"

"Yeah," Sophie said. "He wants me to go back to Maine with him." She laughed, as if this were funny. "What a nut!"

I remembered that Betsy had said Sophie's father wanted to take her home. I guess he was just waiting for Maggins to let her go. And now there I was, practically kidnapping her. The reality of what I was doing was slowly starting to sink in.

We drove on. Sophie fiddled with the dials on the radio. The Christian fundamentalist station came on again. A preacher was talking about walking with the devil. Sophie laughed. "Can you believe this guy?" she said.

I smiled like it was funny, too, but inside I was thinking, *Yeah, I can believe this guy. He's talking about me.*

Then, there it was—the Beeswax Inn. We pulled into the parking lot.

I could see the place in the wall where they'd

---

rebricked the hole I'd made with the dean's Peugeot. Sophie was looking at it, too.

"You did it again, didn't you?" Sophie said, before we opened the doors.

"What?"

"You rescued me," she said quietly. "If you hadn't come, I don't know what would have happened to me. I'd have died in there, I think. Just like that poor hummingbird."

"I don't know," I said. "This isn't really a rescue."

It suddenly occurred to me that I didn't really have much of a plan for what to do with Sophie once I got her out of Maggins and we spent some time together in the Beeswax Inn. I mean, I definitely wasn't going to bring her back to Maggins. But it wasn't like I was planning to take her back to Florida with me, either. We were both just sitting there, in the car, with our seat belts still on.

"Can I ask you a question?" she said.

"Sure."

"Why me, Jonah?"

I looked down at the steering wheel. If someone else had asked me, say Dr. LaRue or Posie had said, "Why Sophie?" I would have said, because I think I'm in love with her. But Sophie was asking me herself, and I wasn't sure of the answer anymore. I sat there in the car and looked out the window at the place where I'd driven through the wall, and wondered how on earth I'd gotten there. It seemed like a dream. I mean, I'd daydreamed about Sophie so many times and thought so much about her. But now that I was actually with her I almost felt like I was with a stranger. I didn't know what to say.

"I don't know," I said.

"But you must know," Sophie said. She sounded kind of disappointed, like I'd given the wrong answer. "It's like you're my guardian angel. What did I ever do to deserve you?"

"I can't explain it," I said to her. But then I gave it a try. "Since the first time I saw you, I sort of felt like I had to look out for you."

"When was that?" she asked.

"You were painting in the art studio," I told her. "You were doing this painting of a girl by a cliff, about to jump."

"Oh, yeah!" Sophie said, remembering. "That was you? Hey, I could have sworn that was Sully."

I clutched the steering wheel, my knuckles were white. "Sully?" I said. "You mean Sullivan the Giant? My old roommate?"

Sophie shrugged like it was no big deal that she was talking about Sullivan like he was this cool guy we both liked. And calling him *Sully*.

—■—

"Yeah. Sully's always loved my painting, I don't know why. He's just really interested in art, you know?"

I looked out at the gray sky. It looked like it might start snowing any minute. It seemed like another world, out there, outside the car.

"I heard he's back at Masthead," I said, coolly. I turned to look at her, but I couldn't read her face at all.

"Yeah," Sophie said, her voice suddenly tired. "He's back all right."

I said the next sentence as slowly as I could. "So, you're in touch with him, then?"

Sophie took my hand. I think she was catching on. "No, no," she said. "I don't know anything about him. Just what I hear from people, you know?"

She was lying to me, I was sure of it. Betsy Donnelly said Sophie and Sullivan were e-mailing each other all the time. I felt so confused. I hated to think that Sophie was lying and I wanted to believe that she wasn't. But I trusted Betsy, and I didn't trust Sophie at all.

"You remember how I told you once I was going to have to save your life sometime, Jonah?" Sophie said.

"Uh-huh."

She reached into her purse and put on some lip

---

gloss. She looked at herself in the passenger side vanity mirror, and then smiled at me. She looked fantastic, but a voice in my head said, *Don't do it, Jonah. She's not for real.*

"Come on," Sophie said, taking my hand. "Let's do it." Then she leaned over and kissed me and the kiss tasted like cherries from her lip gloss. She put her hand behind my head and we stayed where we were, just kissing. I couldn't stop.

In some ways, it was the saddest moment of my life. I was kissing Sophie at last, but I knew she had just lied to me. I knew things weren't right. And I knew I should take her back to Maggins and just get on with my life. But I couldn't stop. I'd wanted this too badly for too long.

We got out of the car and walked arm in arm toward the motel. About halfway across the parking lot, a helicopter flew by overhead. Sophie looked up and her face convulsed with fear for just a second. Then she looked relieved.

"That's not one of the black ones," she said.

I went up to the front desk and I got us a room. The guy behind the counter looked like the kind of guy you'd see reading porno magazines in the back of a news shop. He was hugely overweight, wearing a dirty T-shirt and this gross little goatee. He entered our names into his cruddy computer, and

———■———

we got a key and walked down the hallway and went into our room.

It was the same room she'd been in last year with Sullivan. You could tell from the wall.

(Later.)

Man oh man. This is hard to write.

So there we were. Sophie was sitting on the bed. I was sitting on the bed next to her. I had the condoms in my wallet.

Some color had come back into Sophie's cheeks. She didn't look so crazy now. She looked beautiful. That little voice in my head kept saying, *Don't do it Jonah. She's not for real.* But I ignored it. I was determined to put all my worries aside and just dive in. I was living on the edge.

I took my shirt and my pants off and climbed into bed next to her. Sophie had all her clothes on when she first got under the covers, but she started wriggling around, and soon her pants and her T-shirt were on the floor. I put my arms around her and we started kissing. It felt like a dream, like the dream I'd had over and over for months. Every now and then we'd stop kissing and look at each other, and she was smiling at me like she was just as happy as I was. She wasn't going to burst into tears like she had in Orlando. And she wasn't going to run away. She wanted me, and I wanted her, and it was going happen. I was going to do it for the first time with Sophie, who really mattered to me. She wasn't just any old girl.

Sophie reached down under the covers and wriggled around some more and then she turned to me and said, "Okay, I'm naked."

And all I could think in response was, *I wonder if she's lying.*

"You're amazing," I said, but then it was me who was lying. She wasn't amazing. She was this totally mixed up, confused girl, and I was about to mix her up even more. What was I doing? How could I do it?

"I'm so glad it's you," she said.

"It's me?" I repeated.

"That I'm doing it with for the first time. I feel so lucky it's you, Sul— Jonah."

She was going to call me Sully! Just like that time I'd called Posie "Sophie" by mistake. Sophie had just done the same thing!

Except she hadn't. The more I thought about it, the surer I was that I'd misheard her. I decided not to be an idiot. There I was with Sophie, and there was nothing standing between us except my underwear, which I took off. I got out a condom and put

———■———

it on. *Don't do it Jonah*, the voice repeated. I ignored it.

I held Sophie in my arms and she pressed her face into mine and said, "I love you, Jonah."

"I love you, too, Sophie," I said back.

But as I said the words I knew I was lying. And I knew I wasn't going to be able to go through with it.

There was the sound of another helicopter. The room felt cold all of a sudden. Snowflakes ticked against the window pane. Sophie got out of the bed and stood looking out the window at the snow. She looked pale and unreal silhouetted in the light.

Then she turns to me and she is beautiful and warm and daisies blow through the open window. "Jonah," she says, and she is the way I have always imagined her. With soft, golden hair and a radiant smile. She is sitting in the cockpit of her airplane and the wind is blowing her hair around. Then I blinked and I could see the knobs of her spine as she shivered in the cold, still staring out the window at the bleak winter sky. Her underwear was still on. It was white, and the elastic was slightly frayed. It made her look more fragile than ever. I wanted the other Sophie to come back. The warm, golden one who flew planes and smelled like daisies. The one I was in love with.

—■—

Except she wasn't real.

The real Sophie turned around, her face pinched, and said, "I wish those stupid helicopters would just leave us alone."

And that's when I made my decision.

(Still Feb. 5, even later.)

Okay. So here's what happened:

"Oh, damn," I said to Sophie and sat up in bed. I reached for my underwear and put it back on underneath the covers.

"What?" she said.

"There's something I wanted you to have," I said. "A special present. It's in the car. I'll be right back."

"You're kidding," Sophie said. "Come on. Let's just do it now. I've waited too long."

"No," I said, pulling my pants back on. "I have to get this. Hang on."

"Whatever it is, I don't want it," Sophie said, flopping back down on the bed again and crawling under the covers. "I want you, Jonah."

"You'll always have me," I said. I pulled my shirt on over my head, and put my coat on. I think she knew what I was doing. She just watched me go to the door.

———■———

"Jonah!" she said as I opened it.

"What?"

"You'll always have me, too," she said. I nodded.

Then I went out into the hallway down to the front desk. I looked at my watch. It was quarter to twelve. I passed by all the other rooms in the Beeswax Inn and wondered who else was staying there and what they were doing. It was the kind of place where anything could happen

I got to the front desk, and there was the big sleazy guy again. He was reading an issue of *X-Men.*

"Can I use your phone?" I asked.

"Sorry," he said, barely looking up. "It's private."

"Yeah, well, it's an emergency," I said.

"Sorry," he said, although I could tell he wasn't.

"Listen, it's very important," I said. "I'm not kidding. This really is an emergency."

The guy looked up this time and pointed at me. "And I'm telling you, dude. It's private. Use the phone in your room!"

"I can't use that one," I said.

"Why, is it broken?"

"No," I said. "I just can't use it. I need to use your phone. Now."

"Are we gonna have a problem here, dude?" he said.

I felt Max's metal ball in my coat pocket, and

———■———

my hand closed around it. "I don't think there's going to be a problem," I said. I barely even recognized my voice, I sounded so confindent. I grabbed the man's shirt collar with my other hand and stared him in the eyes. "You're just going to let me use the phone," I told him.

"Jesus. Okay, man, okay!" he said, backing away. "Use the damn phone! Use it all you want!"

I picked up the phone but it started making this weird beeping sound.

"Dude, you gotta hit nine to get an outside line," he told me, shaking his head.

I tried again, and then got information. "Hello?" I said. "Yes. In Philadelphia please. The number for the Morgan Hotel. On City Line Avenue."

They gave me the number and I hit One to have the number automatically dialed. I'd never done that before; it had always seemed like a waste of money.

They connected me to the Morgan Hotel, and I asked to be connected to the line of Mr. O'Brien, and soon Sophie's father answered the phone.

"Mr. O'Brien?" I said.

"Yes?"

"This is Jonah Black."

"Jonah Black," he said, slowly. Sophie's father had this rich Yankee accent. I'd heard his voice once before, when I'd called Sophie's number during Thanksgiving break. Mr. O'Brien had answered the phone and I'd hung up.

"What can I do for you, Jonah?" he said.

"You know who I am?" I said.

"Oh, yes," he said, sadly. "The name Jonah Black is well known in our house."

"Sophie isn't in Maggins anymore. She's in a motel called the Beeswax Inn. It's about a mile west from the Morgan on City Line. She wants—"

My voice broke, and my throat seemed to close right up. The guy at the hotel desk was watching me carefully, listening to the whole conversation.

"She wants you to come get her," I said, quickly. "She wants to come home. She wants to go back with you to Maine. Right now."

There was a long silence on the other end of the line.

"All right then, Jonah," Mr. O'Brien said, almost kindly. "Thank you for calling me."

"Thank you," I said, inexplicably. And then I hung up.

"Thank you," I told the guy behind the desk.

"Sure, man," he said. I think he was glad he was getting rid of me.

"Okay, then," I said. "Thanks again." And then I walked out.

I got into the car and started it up. As I pulled out of the parking lot, I looked back at the room, half hoping that Sophie would be there at the window, waving to me as I drove away. But our room was dark.

On the way back to Dad's house I drove past Maggins. Sullivan the Giant was walking up the front steps, holding a bouquet of flowers. I took the metal ball out of my pocket and kissed it.

I hope she's okay.

(Still Feb. 5, later.)

Well, that's pretty much the whole story of what happened in the Beeswax Inn. Even looking back at it now, it seems like a dream.

I got back to Dad's house and Honey was standing in the front yard, looking kind of anxious. "Hey, Studly," she said quickly. "Listen. Pack up your stuff. We're heading out in an hour, okay?"

"We are? How come?" I was kind of looking forward to soaking in Dad's Jacuzzi, eating a whole lasagna, and sleeping for twelve hours. I felt like I needed to unwind.

"Trust me," Honey said. "It's time to go."

"Where's Max?"

"Max went back to Harvard," she said, sadly.

—■—

"How come?"

"Jonah," Honey said. "He's got, like—classes?"

"Oh, right," I said. I had forgotten that one of the things you actually did at Harvard was go to class. I was starting to think that all anybody did there was hack into computers and play with toy guns.

"All right," Honey said, her eyes shifting toward the house. "So go get ready, okay?"

"What are you doing?" I asked. She definitely looked like she had something up her sleeve.

Honey grinned. "Something fun," she said.

It didn't take me long to get my stuff out of my room. As I packed up I noticed a few cans of paint, standing in the corner. Tiffany was getting started with her redecorating. The name of the color on the side of the can was Roasted Eggplant. We were getting out of there just in time.

I went back outside and loaded my stuff into the Jeep.

Dad came out and watched me pack up. My arm hurt as I put the things in the car, and I thought about asking Dad for help. But I didn't.

"You learning what you need to know down there in Pompano Beach?" he said finally.

"I guess so," I said. He took a sip of his coffee.

"Well," he said.

—■—

"Well."

"It's nice how everything turns out for the best, isn't it?" he said.

I tried to think of something that had turned out for the best. I guess Honey meeting Max was kind of nice. For her.

"Yeah," I said.

"Your sister, going to Harvard. You, a diving star. Your mother, a radio personality and a best-selling author to boot. I'm proud of my family, Jonah, damn proud!"

I thought about telling him how things really were, but I decided to let him enjoy the moment instead. I almost wondered if he was going to hug me.

Then, from upstairs, I heard a scream. It was Tiffany.

Dad looked up at his bedroom window.

Tiffany screamed again.

Dad headed inside, but he didn't seem like he was in too big of a hurry. In fact, he paused to take little sips of his coffee as he trudged up the front steps. I kind of felt sorry for Dad, all of a sudden. He hadn't mentioned himself when he'd talked about all the things that had turned out for the best.

Honey came barreling out the front door. "See ya, Daddy-O," she said.

"Honor—" said Dad. He looked like he wanted to say something to her.

—— ■ ——

"I gotta go," Honey said. She lifted her chin and gave him a quick peck on the cheek. "'Bye."

"Honor, wait," said Dad. "Honey—"

It was the first time he'd ever called her Honey, at least as far as I knew.

Tiffany wailed mournfully from upstairs. I couldn't imagine what Honey had done.

"Go on inside, Dad," said Honey. "You're needed in there."

Dad ducked inside and Honey ran down the walk and jumped into the Jeep. A we roared down the driveway I looked back at Dad's huge house. Dad hadn't gone upstairs after all. He was standing on the porch, waving as we drove away.

A moment later we were heading through Gladwynne, listening to Max's band on the CD player.

I noticed that Honey's hands were all purple.

"Honey," I said. "What happened to your hands?"

The corners of Honey's mouth turned up, wickedly.

"Oh no," I said. "What did you do?"

She snickered, grabbed a Camel from out of her bag, and punched in the lighter. "Dyed her dog," Honey said.

I couldn't help but smile. "You dyed Cuddles?"

"Yup," she said. "Dyed him Royal Velvet."

"What's that?" I said. It sounded like one of Tiffany's paint colors.

—■—

Honey took a drag of her cigarette. "Bright purple. He looked pretty cool, actually."

I sat back in my seat and watched the telephone poles zip by through the window. "Wow, Honey," I said.

"Honor," she said. "I'm going to start using Honor. Max says it's a name with character."

I smiled.

I don't know if Honey needs any more character, but I'll try to call her Honor from now on.

Feb. 9. Baker, Tennessee

We're stopped here at a Motel 6 for the night. I have to say I'm looking forward to getting home.

I've been thinking a lot about Molly. Maybe she was right when she said that sex doesn't matter. Does it matter as much as being with somebody who likes you and cares about you? I wish I hadn't screwed things up with her. I guess I've screwed up with a lot of girls. But now that I really am over Sophie—or maybe she's over me—I think things are going to be better.

While we were driving south, we turned on the radio at one point and there was this girl right in the middle of describing her orgasm. "It's like a wave in the ocean lifting me up and colors bursting in the sun." And then this woman's voice said,

—— ■ ——

"That's good, you shouldn't be ashamed of that! You're only being nice to yourself!" Honey—I mean, Honor—and I looked at each other and said in unison, "Mom!"

Here we are, hundreds of miles from home, and there's Mom on her radio show talking about sex.

And I got this e-mail on the laptop when I logged on from the Motel 6:

To: JBlack94710
From: Northgirl999

Jonah, I can't wait for you to come back. Everything is so boring and stupid without you. I have this funny feeling you are going to be different when you come back, like you will finally have learned something. By now things have probably blown up with Sophie and you've realized that she's the same as anybody else, except maybe she's more lost. I think this is probably going to break your heart, when you realize that Sophie isn't some fantasy-perfect chick, but I think having your heart broken is probably good for you.

That's how people learn, Jonah. Little Mister Wooden Head.

I think I'm ready to reveal myself to you now.

—■—

Feb. 11

I'm home after my first day back at Don Shula. Since I've already done eleventh grade once, it doesn't seem like I missed anything.

We pulled into Pompano Beach around 8:30 A.M., and we thought it would be funny if we just went straight to school, like we hadn't been away at all.

As soon as I walked into Miss von Esse's homeroom, all these girls kept coming up to me and asking questions or stealing furtive looks at me from across the room. I guess Northgirl was right; there were a lot of rumors about me flying around.

Yvonne Wainwright came right up to me and said, "Were you in L.A.? I used to live in L.A. My dad used to be a screenwriter, you know. Did you ever see that movie *Getting Out*? My Dad wrote that. Well, he wrote the first draft. After that some big studio—"

Yvonne speaks about a hundred words a second and while she talks, she moves her hands around like she's interpreting herself for the hard of hearing.

"Yvonne," I said, interrupting her. "I wasn't in L.A."

She looked surprised. "You weren't?"

"No. I was in Pennsylvania, seeing my father."

"So you're not going to UCLA?" Yvonne said. "You aren't diving for them?"

"I don't know," I said. "We have a whole other year till college."

"Well, you should think about it," Yvonne said. "It's a good school."

Over in the corner there was this sudden burst of laughter, and Cilla Wright and her little group of girls looked over at me. Cilla was blushing. Then Cecily La Choy came over and said, "Jonah, everybody says you got married. That's not true, is it?" She looked at me with this urgent expression, like the answer was really important to her.

"No, I didn't get married," I told her. "I didn't even get engaged."

Cecily looked thrilled. "That's what I thought," she said, triumphantly.

"Actually, it's more like I got divorced," I said. And, when I thought about it, that's kind of what it felt like, leaving Sophie behind. For good.

———■———

"Oh," said Cecily, nodding like this made sense to her, when it couldn't have.

Then Linda Norman came over with her white jeans and white tube top and gold earrings and white nail polish.

She looked me up and down. "I can't believe they let you out," she said, popping her gum.

"Out?" I said.

She looked at me like I was trying to hide something, but she knew better. "Like, on parole," she said.

I just shrugged and sat down at my desk, wondering what she thought I'd done.

Just then Thorne walked by the open door of my homeroom, on his way to the Zoo. He saw the crowd of girls around my desk, and gave me the thumbs-up.

I think I'm going to have to murder Thorne. Then I'll really have to go to jail.

When Honor and I got home, Mom and Mr. Bond were on the living room floor sitting cross-legged with their eyes closed. It was like they hadn't moved the whole time we'd been gone. Mr. Bond had his hands on mom's breasts again, and Mom had her hands on Mr. Bond's breasts, which are pretty big for a guy.

"Oonnngggg," Mr. Bond chanted.

"Hi, Mom, Hi, Mr. Bond," I said.

"Jonah," said Mom, opening one eye. "We were just getting tranquil."

Honor looked at me and shook her head. "Hiya, Ma," she said.

"Honey," Mom said, and closed her eye.

"It's Honor, Ma," said Honor.

"It is?" Mom opened her eye again, suspicious.

We left them there and headed down the hallway to our bedrooms. Before I went into my room I said, "Hey, Honor. Thanks for the road trip. I needed that."

Honor tossed her suitcase on her bed and turned around, "I know," she said. "Thanks for keeping me company. Who knows, maybe someday you'll get your own driver's license, and you can drive *me* around. You might want to cruise up to Harvard next fall and check it out. Me and Max can show you around."

"Okay," I said. "Will you tell Max thanks for me?" I said. "If you're in touch with him?"

Honor went over to her bed and unzipped her suitcase. "I'm definitely gonna be in touch with him," she said.

"An eye for an eye, a kiss for a kiss!" said Electra, from inside the suitcase.

AMERICA ONLINE MAIL

To: Northgirl999

From: JBlack94710

Northgirl, who are you?????

—■—

Feb. 14

I came home today and in the kitchen there was a big box of chocolate hearts with a string attached to the bottom and a card that said HAPPY VALENTINE'S DAY, JONAH. LOVE, MOM AND ROBERE. Nobody else was home. Cool, I thought. A surprise gift from Mr. and Mrs. Tranquility. I wondered what I was going to find on the other end of the string. Maybe a new computer. Or an electric guitar. Or a telescope.

So I followed the string down the hall, into my room, out the sliding glass door, into the backyard.

And there, standing on the dock, was a brand new Schwinn. Light blue. With three gears.

Gee, Mom. What a great present. If I was eleven years old, I'd really love it. Still, I guess it was pretty cool of her. She tries.

—■—

Feb. 15

Well, here's the e-mail I got this morning, from guess who:

Jonah! Are you all right?

I wanted to say I'm sorry, but you already know I'm sorry. I guess you know me pretty well, Jonah, better than anyone.

Anyway, I'm back in Maine. It feels good to be home.

I'm sorry if I disappointed you or anything. I'm sorry about everything.

You're still my hero.

Love forever,
Your Sophie

I felt so relieved when I finished reading that. I think I was afraid Sophie was going to tell me she'd

—■—

escaped from her father and now she was hitchhiking South to see me or something. It was a relief to hear the she was okay, home safe.

I thought about Sophie walking by the ocean in Maine, looking out at the lighthouse blinking in the fog. A plane flies by overhead, but she's not on it. Maybe Sophie's going to be all right, taking a little time away from everything. I hope so, anyway.

—■—

Feb. 16

I found the picture of our whole family on vacation, the one that Honor said doesn't exist. Mom, Dad, me, and Honor are all standing around some stalactites and behind us is the sign that says MAMMOTH CAVES.

It's actually a very sweet picture. Honor looks like this perfect little girl, in pigtails and a little pink dress with a big red strawberry on the front. I remember when she used to be like that, like a million years ago.

I took the picture into her room and I said, "Honor, look at this. Remember when you said we didn't take this vacation? Here's a picture."

Honor looked at the picture for a long time. Then she handed it back to me. I said, "Well?"

And she said, "That's not me."

—■—

Feb. 17

Today I was riding by First Amendment Pizza on my new light blue three-speed bike, and suddenly Mr. Swede came running out onto the sidewalk.

"Yonah!" he cried, "Yonah!"

I stopped and looked at him. His apron was covered with sauce. There seemed to be more gray hair at his temples. He was sweating more than usual.

"What's up, Mr. Swede?" I said.

"Come," he said, flapping his hand at me. I leaned my bike against a fire hydrant and Mr. Swede nodded at it approvingly. He ushered me inside, and said, "First Amendment, losing shirt."

"I'm sorry," I told him.

"Come back," he said. "Yonah deliver pizzas. Deliver videos. Deliver DVDs!"

* * *

"DVDs?" He didn't used to have DVDs.

"What about Doober?" I said. "I thought he was working for you."

"Dooba in jail," Mr. Swede said, shaking his head in sorrow.

"Okay," I said. "I'll work for you again, Mr. Swede. But only twice a week, okay?" I wanted to keep my options open.

"Good boy, Yonah," said Mr. Swede. He handed me a stack of videos. "Make delivery now. Yonah Black, Dependable Boy!"

I took the videos and cycled up to Federal Avenue to start delivering them. I kind of liked being Dependable Boy, even though I felt like a loser riding a three-speed.

The first tape I had to drop off was *Pretty Woman*, and it was going to a house near the airfield. I passed the Goodyear Blimp Base, and noticed that the blimp was still missing. What had happened to it? It had been gone for weeks now.

Then, about a half a mile later, I suddenly put the brakes on and stopped cold.

There, on the corner, were the remains of a seedy bar. There'd been a fire, and the place was charred and falling down. The windows were all boarded up. There was glass on the sidewalk.

There was a sign, half-burnt. *THE F*— it read.

—■—

I remembered the match book the Indian girl had dropped when I chased her through the parking lot at our last diving meet.

The Fur Room? I wondered.

Of course, there was no way of knowing what the name of the place had been. It might have been The Firehouse, or The Front Porch, or The Fantastic House of Chicken.

I wondered for a second whether the girl who'd dropped the matchbook really existed at all, or if I'd imagined her, just like I imagined Sophie, in a way.

I bicycled onward feeling sad and happy at the same time. I delivered *Pretty Woman* to a pretty ugly dude cooking Polish sausages in his backyard. I headed back down Federal Highway. The palm trees swayed in the wind. It was good to be home.

Feb. 18

Today I got a second job working on Thorne's dad's boat, the *Scrod*. The good news is that Posie and Thorne are working on the boat, too, which makes it more like having fun than having a job. Most of the time, Thorne and his Dad are the ones catching and gutting fish. I get to steer the boat, which is totally cool. Posie is first mate, which means she lies around on the deck in her orange bikini reading *Wahine* magazine.

I agreed I'd work one day a week, on Saturdays, as long as Posie and Thorne were there, too.

I made pretty good money—$120 for the day! Now I will actually have some extra money for stuff, like going out. Except that I don't have anyone to go out with.

———■———

When we were on the boat Thorne said, "So what's up with Molly Beale?"

"I don't know," I said, keeping my eyes fixed on the horizon. I was trying not to run over any sailboats. "I was thinking I should call her. So we can talk. You know, work things out."

"Talk?" Thorne said. "Are you insane, Jonah? Forget it, man. You got your troops out of there. You keep them out. You have the advantage."

"Since when are girls like, a country you have to invade with troops?" I asked.

Thorne scratched his goatee and laughed. "Since, like, the beginning of the universe."

"And you think I need to keep my troops out of her territory?" I said, going along with his little metaphor.

"Definitely," Thorne said. "If you send in your peacekeepers, they're gonna get blown up. It's a disaster waiting to happen."

I looked over at Thorne. He was wearing a Hawaiian shirt, basketball shorts, a gross fish-gut-stained white apron, and black rubber boots. He looked completely ridiculous.

I steered the boat around a catamaran with luffing red sails. "You know what, Thorne? I actually don't have a clue what you're talking about."

"Jonah," Thorne said, rolling his eyes like I was an

imbecile. "You ditched her. Then she came back and apologized to you. Girls aren't supposed to do that."

"They aren't?"

"No. C'mon man. It's against the Geneva Convention. Apologies are for dudes."

"Why?" I said.

" 'Cause we're the ones who always screw things up," he said, grinning like an idiot.

"Well, I don't know, Thorne. Don't you think I should like, give Molly one more chance?"

"Hello?! Dude, are you listening?" Thorne shouted. "No way. If I was you, I'd maintain the Code of Silence."

"Huh?" He was speaking in code again. The Thorne Wood Code of Nonsense.

"If you call her up, it's just giving her the chance to yell at you," Thorne said. He shook his head. "I don't know about you, man, but I got enough girls calling me up to yell at me. That's why I got caller ID."

Thorne's Dad came up on deck and stood there wiping his hands on a towel. He was wearing a fish-gut-stained apron, too. It's practically the only outfit I've ever seen him in.

"How's it going, boys?" said Mr. Wood.

"Good," we said.

Mr. Wood looked out at the horizon. "Hold her steady, Jonah," he said.

—■—

We rocked on the waves in silence for a while as I held her steady. The boat smelled like fish and gasoline. There was static on the radio. Posie was sitting on a lawn chair up in the bow, wearing sunglasses and her orange bikini. She turned a page of her magazine and took a sip of her Coke.

"Anyway," Thorne said quietly. "You don't have to worry about Molly Beale being lonely. I heard there are a lot of guys interested in her."

"There are?" I said, surprised.

"Oh, yeah," Thorne said, and raised his eyebrows.

Posie got out of her folding chair and spread out a white beach towel on deck and lay down on it. She turned her back to us, untied the top of her bikini, and lay down on her stomach. She had no tan lines whatsoever.

Mr. Wood, Thorne, and I stood there behind the wheel looking at Posie, sunning herself.

"Steady, Jonah," Mr. Wood said. "Steady."

—■—

Feb. 19

I called Molly. I know Thorne told me it was a violation of the Geneva Convention or whatever, But I still wanted to call her. I felt bad that I never e-mailed her back when she wrote me to say she was sorry. Anyway, I called her, but all I got was her answering machine.

Later on, I got on my brand-new light blue bike with only three gears and I rode down to Molly's house. It's a pretty nice house in a nice neighborhood. There's a pool out back surrounded by an ivy-covered white fence. The SUV was parked almost horizontally in her driveway. There were a bunch of ruts in her front lawn and most of her parents' bushes were crushed or broken. Good old Molly. I love what a lousy driver she is. It's my favorite thing about her.

—■—

I was just about to stop and push my bike up to the front door when I saw Thorne and Molly come out of the house together.

Molly got behind the wheel of the SUV and Thorne got in the passenger side. She revved the engine up, but they didn't go anywhere. I could see them kissing through the back window. Then the reverse lights came on. I made a U-turn and rode on my bike in the opposite direction.

Good old Thorne.

At first I wanted to be mad at him and mad at Molly, too. She was always telling me what a bullshit artist Thorne was and criticizing my taste in friends. But as I pedaled and pedaled with the warm Florida wind on my face I didn't feel mad. I didn't really mind at all.

I biked down to the beach and dumped the bike against the wall of Miller's Pharmacy. I didn't even lock it. If somebody wanted to steal the bike, I really wouldn't mind. I walked down the beach to the lifeguard tower and climbed up. There were a few people hanging out on the Dune, but I didn't feel like going over there.

I needed to think. I needed to think about what was next.

At that moment, there was a voice below me, and I looked down, and of course it was Pops Berman.

—■—

"Hi, Pops," I said. "You coming up?"

"I can't climb that damn thing anymore," he shouted. "Come on, Chipper. You come down."

I didn't move right away. I kind of wanted to be alone.

"Come on down here, goddammit," he croaked. "So I can yell at you."

"Pops, I'm really not in the mood, okay?"

"Well, I'm not in the mood, either. You know I'm gonna croak any goddamn second now? I got a liver like a piece o' Swiss cheese. I got a pancreas like a snot rag. My bowels are like—" He paused, out of breath. "My bowels are no damned good!"

I got up and climbed down the lifeguard tower. The wind was pretty fierce and I was afraid it was going to blow the old man over. He was wearing his Red Sox cap. I could smell peanut butter on his breath.

"I'm sorry about your liver, Pops," I said. "And your bowels."

He pointed his cane at me. "You haven't done it, have you?"

"What?" I said. But I knew what he was going to say.

"Walked your doggy!" he shouted. "Made him stand up and bark!"

I just buried my face in my hands. "No, Pops," I said.

"You know why?" he said. "Because you're stupid! "

"I'm not stupid!" I yelled back at him. Suddenly, I'd had enough of him, of everybody. I was really angry. "I'm just trying to live my life."

Pops shook his head. "Running around the country like a bus driver. It's pathetic."

"Why don't you leave me alone, okay?" I said, kicking at the sand that was seeping into my shoes.

"Because," Pops said, out of breath. "I like you, Chipper. I'm trying to give you some advice."

The wind blew his hat off. I was about to go get it, but Pops ran and grabbed it, and scooped it up in his hands with this sudden burst of energy that made me think, whoa, he really *was* a shortstop. He stuck the cap back on his head and came back to me, his chest heaving.

"Had to get my topper," he muttered and squinted at me. "What were we doing here? Oh, yeah. I was giving you advice."

"Every time I follow your advice I wind up in trouble," I told him.

Pops shook his head in disdain. "You've never followed my advice, Chipper," he said. "Not once!"

"What do you mean?" I said. I'd been trying to walk my doggy for months. And I'd gotten burned every time.

—■—

"What are you doing chasing around all these ghosts when you've got the right girl right in front of your face?" Pops said.

"What?" I said. There wasn't anyone in front of my face except Pops.

Pops shook his head crossly. "Open your eyes, Chipper," he said.

"Okay," I said, although I still didn't know what he was talking about. I didn't think he did, either.

"You don't have to do it with her," he said. "All you gotta do is notice her."

Suddenly the wind blew his hat off again and this time Pops reached out, quick as a cat, and caught it in one hand. He looked at the hat for a moment, then he reached forward and put it on my head.

"You wear that for a while," he said. "Maybe it'll bring you some luck."

The hat fit me perfectly. He had probably worn it when he played in the majors, decades ago. It was a really good gift.

"Thanks, Pops," I said. "Thanks."

I started to walk away from him. But then he called after me. "Chipper!" he shouted.

I turned back. "What?"

"The other way," he said, and pointed with his cane toward the Dune. "That way."

———■———

How did he know where I was supposed to go? I wondered. But then, there's always been something about Pops Berman that makes me wonder if he's really my guardian angel, or an alien, or something. As far as I know, nobody other than me has ever seen him.

"Okay," I said, and as I walked past him, heading toward the Dune, he patted me on the shoulder.

"You're going to be all right now, Chipper," he said. "You are."

I walked up the beach feeling really strange. Part of me felt more alone and loserish than ever, but I also felt like something great was about to happen. Maybe it was Pops's hat that made me feel that way, I don't know. I felt like a fly ball was going to drop down out of the sky and fall perfectly into my glove.

I took off my shoes and walked in the cold, cold surf. It gave me goose bumps, but it felt raw and real. I was wide awake.

As I walked toward the Dune, I saw someone standing up on top of it, looking up at the sky. There was a strange whining sound. As I drew closer, I saw it was Posie, wearing a blue windbreaker and white jeans, looking up at her plane, circling and diving.

I thought about how Pops had told me to open

■

my eyes, and how he'd shoved me in the direction of the Dune. And I thought, Posie, of course. It made complete sense.

I stood there watching her flying her plane for a while and I walk toward her and say her name, "Posie." She turns to me and her eyes open wide and she smiles her golden smile. When she says my name, "Jonah," it's like I'm hearing what my name actually sounds like for the very first time.

The biplane slowly flies out to sea, and she steps toward me and puts her arms around my neck and now we are kissing and I can smell the ocean in her hair. As we kiss I think how perfectly we fit together, how we have always been two pieces of the same puzzle.

In the surf below me, I can see a white scarf floating on the waves. It is slightly torn and burned.

The buzzing of the plane grew louder and I looked up and saw two planes, circling in the sky. Lamar Jameson came walking over the crest of the Dune and put his hand on Posie's waist. She kissed him and then ducked away to steer her plane into a loop-de-loop.

Pops Berman was wrong. He'd pushed me in the wrong direction.

I turned around and started walking back toward

—■—

the lifeguard tower. I was going to get back to my stupid little bike and head home.

There was no sign of Pops Berman anywhere. A blackboard on the tower said: OCEAN TEMP: 58. WINDS: 15 MPH. WARNING. MAN-OF-WAR. RIPTIDES. UNDERTOWS.

There was a gust of wind, and Pops's hat blew off my head and rolled along the beach behind me like a hubcap. I turned to run after it.

Right in front of me was a girl. She bent down and picked up Pops's hat and put the hat backward on her head. Then she smiled and walked toward me. Her hair was blowing around in the wind and she was wearing a thin black T-shirt. There were goose bumps on her tanned arms.

"Hey, Mr. Wooden Head," said Caitlin Hoff, Posie's little sister.

I felt like I was seeing her for the first time. She had light brown hair, a little curlier than Posie's, and her face was more thoughtful. There was a small vertical line that formed on her forehead like she was thinking hard about something. I wondered if there was a similar line on my forehead.

"Northgirl?" I said.

Caitlin smiled. "Hello, Jonah."

It was funny. We didn't rush forward into each other's arms and start kissing. We didn't strip off all

---

our clothes and lie down in the sand. I didn't get down on one knee and pledge my undying love for her, now that we were together.

What happened was, I had no idea what to say. We just stood there for a moment, quietly, with the wind whipping around us, and the cold February ocean crashing near our feet. It was strange to be with someone who knew me so well, but who I didn't really know at all. She was right. I'd never really noticed her before. I thought Caitlin didn't even like me!

I guess the reason I thought she didn't like me was because I wasn't paying attention.

"What do we do now?" I said, finally.

"I don't know," Caitlin said. "We better figure something out quick, though. I'm freezing."

"Do you want to, um, you know, hang out?" I said. "I mean, do you still like me now that I know who you are?"

She shrugged, and looked almost ashamed. "I'm only in tenth grade," she said. "You're Jonah Black, the diving star, the guy every girl wants to go out with. Do you really want to go out with a tenth grader? With your friend's little sister?"

I thought about it.

Caitlin licked her lips kind of nervously. "Maybe it helps that I know you better than anyone. Better than Thorne. Better than Molly Beale. Better than Posie. Better than Sophie."

I nodded. "Yeah," I said. "I don't know how you know me so well, but you do."

She looked out at the water. "Of course, you don't know beans about me, though, do you, Jonah?" she said.

I shrugged. "Nope."

"So if we hang out, what're we going to talk about?" she asked.

I took a step toward her. "I don't know," I said. "Maybe I could get to know you."

"Uh-huh," she said. She put her hands in her back pockets. "That sounds good. And how are you going to do that?"

I took another step toward her. I liked the way her eyelashes were blond at the tips. "Maybe we could talk," I said. "I could ask you some questions."

She thought it over, like I'd proposed something rare and complicated.

Caitlin took my hand. I kissed her on the cheek. It was absolutely the best kiss in all of Florida history.

Then she said, "Well, what do you want to know?"

"Everything," I said.

—■—

We started to walk down the beach together, still holding hands. The Goodyear blimp suddenly sailed into view. I wondered where it had been all this time.

I looked up at Niagara Towers as we walked by. There was Pops Berman standing on the balcony of his apartment, drinking a glass of milk. I'm pretty sure he was smiling.

I think I'll stop here for now.

Maybe tomorrow I'll start a new journal.